the
DREADFUL
REVENGE
of
ERNEST
GALLEN

Also from Bloomsbury
by James Lincoln Collier

The Empty Mirror

the DREADFUL REVENGE of ERNEST GALLEN

JAMES LINCOLN COLLIER

BLOOMSBURY
CHILDREN'S
BOOKS

Published by Bloomsbury U.S.A. Children's Books
175 Fifth Avenue, New York, New York 10010
Distributed to the trade by Macmillan

Library of Congress Cataloging-in-Publication Data
Collier, James Lincoln.
The dreadful revenge of Ernest Gallen / James Lincoln Collier.—1st U.S. ed.
p. cm.
Summary: When Eugene starts hearing a voice inside his head telling him to do awful
things, it leads him to look into his small town's past before the Depression, and to
discover long-hidden secrets about his neighbors and his town.
ISBN-13: 978-1-59990-220-3 • ISBN-10: 1-59990-220-6
[1. Supernatural—Fiction.   2. Depressions—1929—Fiction.   3. Horror stories.]
I. Title.
PZ7.C678Dr 2008   [Fic]—dc22   2007044453

First U.S. Edition 2008
Typeset by Westchester Book Composition
Printed in the U.S.A. by Quebecor World Fairfield
1 3 5 7 9 10 8 6 4 2

For Gabby

the DREADFUL REVENGE OF ERNEST GALLEN

Chapter 1

Around five o'clock the kids began saying they had to go home, so we quit playing ball for the day. I shouldn't have been playing baseball anyway: I should have spent the afternoon at Snuffy's Groceries to see if I could earn a few dimes making deliveries. But it was too nice an afternoon, the way it can be at the end of May when school's almost out—sun shining, just enough breeze to keep the heat down, a few puffy white clouds drifting along upstairs minding their own business and hoping that everybody else will mind theirs. Couldn't deliver groceries on a day like that.

Sonny Hawkins and I were the last to leave. "You gonna play ball tomorrow?"

"I don't know," I said. "I ought to go over to Snuffy's and see if they've got any deliveries."

"Naw, you don't want to do that, Gene," Sonny said. He was my best friend and said whatever he wanted to me. "Let's play ball."

"I ought to go over to Snuffy's. What are you going to do?"

"If we can't get up a ball game, I might as well go over to the country club and see if I can hook a tennis ball. There's usually a few laying around there."

We used tennis balls to practice baseball with. You could bounce them off the side of a house or something to practice grounders. Or hit them up against a wall, if you could find a good wall. "You're going to get in trouble hooking tennis balls," I said.

"I ain't afraid of them snobs, *Yew*gene," Sonny said.

"What happened to your old tennis ball?"

"I hit it into the river by mistake."

"How come?" Sonny was the best baseball player we had and didn't make too many mistakes in hitting.

"I meant to bunt it, but it was hangin' up

there so fat and juicy I couldn't hold myself back and gave it a wham and it landed in the river. I got to get another one."

"Well, if there aren't any deliveries, I'll go over with you," I said. Sometimes there were, and sometimes there weren't. With times as hard as they were, a lot of people would rather carry their groceries home than have to tip a boy to bring them.

So Sonny headed off for River Road, and I set off along Courthouse Street for home. Right then there wasn't too much wrong with the world that I could see. Sun still shining on my back, cool breeze on my face, the big elms along Courthouse Street waving their leaves just a little in a friendly way. I'd got a couple of nice hits, and was plenty hungry for supper, too.

I was going along that way, humming a little song to myself, when I began to feel a tightening in my chest, sort of like a cramp. Well, not exactly a cramp—more like something was swelling in there. A strange kind of feeling, like nothing I'd ever had before, at least so far as I could remember.

I stopped walking so as to look at it better. It

didn't hurt, exactly, just sort of uncomfortable. I shook myself. Well, it probably wasn't anything. I'd had a liverwurst sandwich Mom had made me for lunch. That might've done it—liverwurst was pretty heavy on the stomach. I took a deep breath and shook myself again. Probably the feeling would go away soon. So I started walking toward home again.

Then something else began to happen. I stopped walking so as to figure it out. The tightness feeling, pressure, whatever you called it, was still there, but now there was some motion inside me, going from one side to the other. Jump a little, bounce again, like a restless animal in a cage looking for something to do. I was starting to feel scared. How could it have got in there? I put my hands on my stomach and felt around, trying to catch whatever was bouncing around in there. I couldn't feel anything, but the tightness and the bouncing went on.

It had to be that sandwich. Maybe if I took a drink of water it would calm things down. I'd better get home as soon as I could. And I started

4

to put a foot forward when from somewhere inside my head I heard a voice. "Hello, Eugene," it said. "I'm glad we finally meet. I've wanted to make your acquaintance for a good while."

I stopped dead, frozen still, feeling sick and cold. My mouth opened, but I couldn't speak. For a minute there was nothing, and I was about to decide that I'd imagined it, when the muffled, hollow voice came again. "Well, Eugene? Aren't you glad to hear from me? We're going to be friends, you know. Or perhaps fellow conspirators is a better way of putting it. Don't be afraid of me. We have to talk."

"You're not real," I said. "I'm just hearing things."

"Oh, yes, I'm real. Real as you are. Can't be seen or touched, that's true, but real nonetheless. You can't see the wind, can you? Can't touch beauty. But they're real all the same."

I felt strange talking to my own insides. I didn't want to do it. "How did you get inside me?"

"For somebody like me that's not a problem," the voice said.

I went on standing there, trying to convince myself that this wasn't happening, that I should ignore the voice, go on home to supper, and forget about it. Maybe if I ignored it, it would stop.

Then the hollow, muffled voice came again. "Yes, of course I've knocked you off balance a little, Eugene. I'm sorry about that, but you'll get used to me."

"What do you want?" I whispered.

"Ah, we'll get to that. I just wanted to introduce myself this time. You'll find out more as time goes along. Don't worry, I'll be back again." There was silence, and then the clenching in my chest started to loosen and the little thing in my stomach slowly quieted down. In a moment it was over.

I stood there, dazed, weak in my legs. I realized that my face was covered with cold sweat, and I wiped it away with my hand. Then I started to run toward home as fast as I could.

Mom was already putting supper on the table—her rule was that supper went on at five thirty and if you were late and got a cold supper, that was your own fault. We sat down—franks and beans with some of Mom's homemade bread-and-butter pickles. I wasn't sure I could eat, since I was still feeling shaky and empty inside. To my surprise, I found myself gobbling up the franks and beans.

"Slow down, Gene," Grampa said. "This isn't a horse race." Grampa was big on proper table manners—big on everything like that, such as using good English, standing up when a lady entered the room, saying "please" and "thank you." Before the Depression Grampa had been a judge, had a big house and plenty of money. I remembered that big house. Mom and I had lived there with him when I was around seven. Big pillars in front and a gravel driveway curving up to them. Then came the hard times and Grampa had lost his job and we moved into this narrow little house. He had a little money saved, just about enough for us to struggle on with, along with what little money Mom made typing for people.

"Sorry," I said. "We played baseball this afternoon and it made me hungry." Generally speaking, I was likely to tell Mom and Grampa whatever had happened to me. Not always— there were some things you wouldn't tell a grown-up. But I got along with them pretty well. Especially Grampa. He'd take me into St. Louis to see the Cardinals play two or three times a year when he could scrape together a few bucks, as he put it. Sometimes we took Sonny, too—his dad wasn't one to go to baseball games. But I didn't want to talk about what had happened that afternoon. Wanted to forget about it, pretend it hadn't happened, make it go away. So I said, "How'd the Cards do yesterday, Grampa?"

"They took care of the Cubs pretty well. Medwick hit a homer." I liked Medwick, but my favorite player was the Cards' third baseman, Pepper Martin.

Sonny Hawkins was our best fielder—best everything in baseball—and naturally he got to play shortstop, so I played second base. We practiced the double play a lot. We'd bounce a ball off the side of Sonny's house and field it until Sonny's mom shouted out that she couldn't stand the thumping on her kitchen. "How many wins is that for Dean now?" I asked, hoping that if I concentrated on baseball the other thing would go away.

Still, I felt kind of shaky and hollow inside. When we finished supper I said that I had homework to do. I washed the dishes, dried them, and put them away. Then I went up to my room. It was pretty small—everything in that house was pretty small. Just room enough for my iron cot bed, a little bureau Mom had got secondhand from the Salvation Army, a little table for my homework, and a chair. Grampa had put hooks behind the door for my clothes so I wouldn't fling them on the chair at night, but mostly I flung them on the chair anyway.

So long as I'd been eating and talking and washing dishes, I'd been able to push away the strangeness of what had happed to me, but now that I was alone, it came back. I felt like I wasn't me anymore, like I'd turned into somebody else—wasn't the same old Eugene Richards I'd been familiar with all my life, but a stranger to myself. I shivered. I decided to work on my science homework in hopes it would take my mind off the feeling. So I sat down at my desk and opened up my science book to Newton's Laws. But I couldn't concentrate: odds and ends of things kept rushing in and pushing Newton's

Laws out of the way. Finally I gave up. I went down to the living room to say good night. Grampa looked at his watch—a big gold watch that had belonged to his own father and was one of the few things he had left. "A little early for you, isn't it, Gene?"

"I just feel tired," I said. And I went to bed. I didn't sleep too well—kept waking up and lying there with thoughts whirling around in my head, but I'd doze off again, and in the morning I felt a little better. The strange feeling had faded out the way a bad dream does, and it faded out some more as the day went on. Maybe it had just been one of those things that happens once and never happens again. Some kind of trick my mind played on itself, like those times when you suddenly have a feeling that whatever you're doing happened before. That was probably it—a trick of the mind, like I had skipped a minute and needed a little time to get back in line with the world.

By the time school was out at three o'clock, I was feeling a good deal more like my regular old Gene Richards. So when Sonny said, "Let's go out to the country club and see if we can hook some tennis balls," I figured I'd do it to show myself I was normal again. We set off on out there along Courthouse Road, past the field where we usually played, and into the countryside. A couple of farms out there, silos, tiny shoots of corn in the field, cows here and there. It was a good ways out to the country club, and to while the time away I said, "Sonny, what do you figure on doing when you grow up?"

"I don't figure on growin' up," he said.

"Don't figure on growing up?" I gave him a look. "How're you going to keep from growing up?"

"Oh, I expect I'll get bigger. I don't see no harm in that. Get big enough so I don't have to take stuff from nobody. But I don't aim on being a grown-up."

Sonny was always having to look after his little sisters, who mostly weren't too clean and had snot dripping down their noses. "I still don't get what's wrong with being a grown-up," I said. "Maybe we could be doctors, make a ton of money, and drive around in new Buicks all the time."

"Naw," he said. "Who wants to be a grown-up?"

"What's wrong with being a grown-up?"

"You ever seen a grown-up you wanted to be like?"

"Sure," I said. "Those guys on the Cardinals—Martin and those."

"They ain't real grown-ups. They're baseball players."

I thought about that for a moment. Sonny didn't do too well in school, but sometimes he saw things that other kids didn't. "Well, maybe. All the same, there are advantages to being a grown-up—no more school, drive a car, carry around a pocketful of money, nobody telling you what to do all the time."

"I don't see a lot of grown-ups with pockets full of money, and besides, I don't do what anyone says anyway."

"It's because of the Depression that nobody has any money," I said. "My grampa doesn't have much money anymore, but he used to have a lot. If he wants to see the Cards, he can go. You and me, we have to wait until somebody takes us."

"Even so, it ain't worth it. What's to admire about grown-ups? You ever see a grown-up tell you the truth about anything? I don't think most of 'em even know what the truth is."

"I figure they tell the truth among themselves," I said. "They have to lie to kids, because they want us to grow up right and not be like them."

"There you are, *Yew*gene. You said it yourself."

I could see that it was a tricky question and I decided not to argue about it. "Do you really think we could get good enough to make the Cards?"

"Sure we can, Gene. All we got to do is practice a lot. That's why we need to get some tennis balls. You know how grown-ups are always telling you to plan for your future? Well, that's what we're doing. We ain't just hooking tennis balls; we're planning for our future."

I didn't feel exactly right about hooking tennis balls. It seemed mighty close to stealing. "Maybe if we asked for a couple of old tennis balls they might give them to us."

"What's the point of it if we don't hook them?" Sonny said. "They got millions of 'em laying around up there. They ought to know better than to leave 'em laying around like that. Somebody might walk off with a couple."

I wasn't sure that answered the question, but I decided to leave it alone. We were coming up to the country club now—big gate with stone pillars, long driveway leading from the gate back to the clubhouse, golf course with a few people here and there swinging golf clubs. We skirted around the gate, cut along the edge of the golf course, and went through some pines where there were three or four tennis courts. Nobody playing. We wandered around, searching the ground. It didn't take me long to realize that there wouldn't be much danger of being caught hooking tennis balls, since there weren't any lying there waiting to be hooked. After about fifteen minutes a groundskeeper came along carrying a rake. "You boys!" he shouted. "Whad'ya think you're doin' here?"

Sonny walked up to him bold as brass, and I followed along. "Mister, we come up to see if you had any jobs for boys."

"Oh," said the groundskeeper. "I doubt it. They ain't lookin' to hire boys when there's grown men out of work. But you could try over there at the caddyshack." He pointed.

"Thanks, mister," Sonny said. We walked over to where the groundskeeper had pointed, still keeping our eyes open for tennis balls, but as soon as we were out of sight we skedaddled out of there. "Whenever you get caught someplace where you don't belong," Sonny said, "always say you were lookin' for a job. I done it a million times. It always works. They think you're a real good kid to be lookin' for work instead of coming out there to hook something."

So we didn't end up with any tennis balls, but I was pretty much back to feeling like my old self. Whatever had happened, it was gone, and had slid into the past. Of course, I should have been delivering groceries. You didn't get paid for it, but the people were supposed to tip you a dime, and maybe more if there were a lot of stairs to climb and the box was heavy. Although sometimes they were poor old folks, or plain cheap, and wouldn't give you but a nickel. The rule was that I gave Mom half of whatever I made toward groceries, and kept half for myself. I was saving up for a new fielder's glove, but we kept having to chip in for new baseballs all the time, because they were cheap and got their covers knocked off pretty easy. You could tape the covers on with electrical tape — if someone's dad had any electrical tape we could hook — but once we'd hit them around a lot the balls got lopsided. You could throw a roundhouse curve three feet wide with a lopsided baseball, but they were pretty hard to field, especially on an old cow field that wasn't too smooth to begin with.

On the whole, I was feeling pretty good when I headed home. And I was only a half mile away from supper when I felt that tightness in my chest, the feeling that something was swelling up in there. My heart sank, and I stopped walking.

Chapter 2

"Go away," I said in a loud voice so it could see I was determined. "I don't want to talk to you." Now I felt that movement inside me—something moving from here to there and back again. "Just go away and leave me alone."

"Gene, Gene," came the hollow, muffled voice inside my head. "That's not the way to talk to a companion."

"I'm not your companion," I said. "Go away."

"Oh, but I'm not going to do that, am I, Gene?"

I still couldn't believe that this was really happening. Surely it was some kind of quirk in my head and would stop after a while. Maybe I could just ignore it. So I started walking toward home again.

There came a kind of throaty chuckle, like a heavy chain rattling. "Can't walk away from our insides, can we, Gene?" it said. "Not possible, is it, Gene."

"I'm ignoring you. I'm not going to listen to you."

It chuckled again. "Not much chance of that, is there, Gene."

Ignoring the voice wasn't going to work, and I stopped walking. I was feeling scared and worried. "You're not real," I said. "You can't be real."

"Real as you are, Gene."

"You can't be. Where are you?"

"Everywhere, Gene. Everywhere and nowhere. Now let's get down to business."

"I'm not going to believe in you," I said. "I don't have to believe in things if I don't want to."

"Not true, Gene. The world wasn't made to suit you. Whether you believe in me or not, I'm here. Now let's stop this arguing. It's rather unpleasant, don't you think?"

What was I going to do? Maybe I could make some kind of a deal with it. "What do you want?"

"Ah, that's more like it, Gene. We have to try to get along. Tell me, Gene, do you like your grampa?"

Grampa? What did Grampa have to do with this? "What do you mean, do I like him?"

"I mean, do you think he's a nice person?"

"Sure he's a nice person. Mom and I would be stuck without him." Mom had gone to secretarial school. She was a good typist and made a little money typing letters and reports for some businessmen—lawyers, real estate agents. But it wasn't enough to keep us. We needed Grampa.

"You get along with him then, Gene."

"Why do you care if I like him?"

"That doesn't answer the question."

What was the voice driving at? "Sure I do. He likes baseball, same as me. He takes me to see the Cards when he can put a few dollars together."

"There are some things you ought to know about your grampa that might change your mind a little bit."

"What?"

"Once upon a time, back when you were a little boy, your dear beloved grampa did something unforgivable. Something that got an innocent man killed. That's the truth, Gene."

"Never," I said. "I don't believe you. You're lying. Why should I believe anything you say?"

"Find out for yourself, then. That little girlfriend of yours can help. What's her name— Sam."

I felt myself blush. It was talking about Alice Samuels. "She isn't my girlfriend. I don't have a girlfriend. She's just a friend."

It chuckled. "Either way," it said. "However you want. She can help you to find out about your grampa."

"How? How can she?"

"Think about it, Gene. Everybody around Magnolia has forgotten about it. But I haven't, and I want to remind them. Oh, yes, we're going to remind them, you and I, Gene."

I thought about that for a minute. "If you know, why don't you tell me?"

"Ah, that won't do. You'd never believe me. You have to see it for yourself."

I thought some more. "If I do it, will you go away?"

"That's part of it. There are one or two other things we need to work out, Gene. Then I'll go. Then you'll be rid of me."

"What are they?" I said.

"One thing at a time, Gene," it said. "One thing at a time." Then I noticed that the tightness in my chest was easing, and the movement inside was slowing down. In a moment it was gone.

I stood there feeling kind of sick and shaky, as if a huge black bird were hovering over my head. What had I done wrong to deserve this? I must have done something, but what was it? Skipping groceries to play baseball sometimes? Not doing my homework here and there? Those weren't big enough things to deserve this. What was it?

And what was I going to do about it? How could Alice Samuels help me? It was true that she was a curious person, always wanting to know the truth behind things. You couldn't make a simple remark to her without getting into a discussion about it. Couldn't even say "It looks like rain," for she wanted to know what looked like rain about it, and how could I tell and such. She got that from her dad, who was editor of the *Magnolia Chronicle*. Her dad used to be a reporter for the *St. Louis Post-Dispatch*, which Grampa always said was a very good newspaper. "A trained reporter has to question everything he's told," Sam always said.

Then it occurred to me: maybe that was why the spirit, the voice, whatever it was, had said she could help me. Maybe whatever had happened back when I was little had come out in the *Chronicle* then. Sam would know how to get the back issues.

Should I do it? It seemed like I had to if I was ever going to get rid of the voice. What kind of excuse could I give Sam? I'd have to think about it. So I walked on home trying to think of some story for Sam. When I got home it was a quarter to six, but Mom hadn't put supper on. Instead, she and Grampa were sitting in the living room, Mom on the sofa, Grampa in his usual chair by the window. I was surprised. "I'm sorry I'm late," I said.

Then I noticed that Mom and Grampa were

looking at me in a funny, quiet way. "Gene," Mom said. "Sonny Hawkins' dad had an accident this morning."

"He had an accident?"

"Yes," Grampa said. "He was working as a temp at the lumberyard. He had two or three days there, filling in for a fellow who was sick. He was up on the top platform handing down two-by-sixes. The man said that all of a sudden he walked off the platform into midair. Walked off like there was solid ground there. They said he might have survived, for it was only a fifteen-foot drop, but a lot of two-by-sixes followed him down and landed on him."

"Might have survived?" I gasped. "He's dead?"

There was a little silence. Then Mom said, "I'm afraid so, Gene. Mr. Hawkins is dead. I think you ought to go see Sonny after supper."

I felt sort of frozen. I never had much to do with Mr. Hawkins. He wasn't around Sonny's house a lot—gone fishing, picked up an odd job, I don't know what. Nobody thought much of him in Magnolia. He wasn't a drinker, didn't hit his wife and children, nothing like that. People said he was bone lazy. Didn't like to work a whole lot and was always thinking up schemes for easy money. "I can't believe he's dead," I said finally.

"It's a shame," Grampa said. "According to the fellows at the lumberyard, he just walked off that platform into midair."

"I think you ought to go see Sonny," Mom said. "I'll get supper on."

I didn't much want to do it. I didn't know what you said when someone died—or how to act, either. Were you supposed to act normal, or were you supposed to be sorrowful and say how much Sonny was going to miss his dad, when he probably wouldn't miss him at all?

But I saw I had to do it. Mom was going to make me, anyway, and she said she'd drive me over to River Road. It would only make it worse to have Mom along, so after supper I set off by myself. The Hawkins' place was on the river, set back a couple hundred feet. Easy for Sonny and me to go skinny-dipping there in the summer. It wasn't much of a place, halfway between a cabin and a real house, with a tin roof that sounded like thunder when it rained, a rickety front porch with an old car seat on it for sitting, kitchen, living room, back room, a couple of little bedrooms upstairs under the eaves. Mr. and Mrs. Hawkins had one bedroom, Sonny's snotty little sisters had the other, so Sonny slept in a corner of the living room that had been closed off with a curtain. Had to do his homework on the kitchen table, which wasn't easy because the radio was usually going and the snotty sisters fighting. Not that it mattered a whole lot, given the amount of homework Sonny was likely to do. No faucet water—pump by the kitchen sink. Grampa said that out there by the river the water wasn't more than five feet down, which was why you couldn't put a cellar under the houses. Soil was so sandy you could drive a three-inch pipe into the ground, screw a pump on the top of it, and you'd have water. If you wanted a bath at the Hawkins' house you had to pump up a tub of water and heat it on the kitchen stove. Sonny didn't take any more baths than he had to, but he managed.

I walked out along River Road and then down the path that led to the Hawkins' place. It was full dark by the time I got there, and there was a light in the kitchen window. I went up to the house, onto the porch, and knocked on the door. A woman's voice I didn't recognize said, "Who is it?"

"Gene Richards," I said. "I'm a friend of Sonny."

The door opened and a strange woman looked out. "He's not at home. They went up to the funeral home to pick out a coffin. Don't know who's going to pay for it. Won't be me. I'm Mrs. Hawkins' sister. I came to comfort the family."

"Oh," I said. "Well tell Sonny that Gene came by. Tell him I'm sorry about his dad. Tell him I'll see him in school tomorrow. We can play ball if he feels like it." Then I remembered my manners. "I mean, please tell him, ma'am." I turned around and left.

But Sonny wasn't in school. I wasn't surprised. He'd got a good excuse for skipping school and was taking advantage of it. I figured he'd work the opportunity for the rest of the week, if his mom didn't get tired of having him around the house.

Seeing as Sonny wasn't likely to be in school

for a while, I knew I'd better go around to see him. After school I walked out to River Road and then down to the Hawkins' place. It was a nice sunny day. I probably should have gone to Snuffy's to see if there were any deliveries, but I knew Mom wouldn't say anything if she knew I'd gone to comfort Sonny instead.

As I came around the corner of the house I found Sonny out front with an old worn-out bat, hitting rocks into the river. He swung and popped the rock straight upwards. "Pop up," I said. "Infield fly rule."

"You startled me coming around the corner like that or I'd have creamed it."

Quickly, I said, "I'm sorry about your dad," so as to get it over with.

He looked at me and then looked away. "Listen, *Yew*gene, my aunt's visiting. She smokes like a chimney. I'll see if I can swipe a couple of ciggies. We can go down by the river and have a smoke." He dropped the bat onto the sandy grass next to the pile of stones he'd collected and went into the house. In a couple of minutes he came out, grinning. "She left her pack by the sink. I got a bunch of 'em."

"You get matches?"

" 'Course I did. You think I'm a dope, *Yew*-gene?"

"Don't be so confident of yourself," I said. "You forgot last time."

We went through the sandy grass down to the river and turned downstream. A couple of hundred yards along, there was a big old willow tree hanging out over the river, its viny branches dangling into the water. Being as it was June, the willow was leafed out. It was a good place to smoke, for the tree trunk was wide enough for us both to rest our backs against, and in under the branches we were hard to spot from any direction. Kind of cozy in there, as a matter of fact.

So we sat down with our backs against the tree and lit up. The day was near perfect. Warm, lots of blue sky with here and there a fluffy white cloud drifting along like a floating elephant. Close to the shore the water swirled and eddied, swinging leaves and twigs around in a rush. Farther out, there were bigger things on the surface: branches, maybe a tree trunk, a straw hat that blew off a boat, maybe even a chair. Always something to see in the river, even if it was only swirls and eddies flashing red and yellow in the sun. Once we even saw a goat standing on an upside-down table in between the legs, bleating away like sixty. Don't know how it got there. We leaped up and raced along the riverbank, hoping we could capture the goat. Would have been fun to have had a goat to fool around with. But with the tangle of trees and roots along the bank we couldn't make much time and the goat got away from us. We heard it bleating for a long while after.

Lazy as we were feeling, there wasn't much need for conversation, but you had to have at least a little, so I said, "Sonny, do you really like smoking? I know it's supposed to be fun and all, and I like watching the smoke come out of my mouth, but for taste I'll take a chocolate soda any day."

"Sure I like it," Sonny said. "I wouldn't smoke if I didn't. It ain't supposed to taste like a chocolate soda. It's supposed to taste sort of rough and miserable, like brown shoe polish. That's the value in it. Smoking wouldn't have any value if it didn't have that brown shoe polish taste to it."

That was Sonny—always seeing things other kids would have missed. But I wasn't going to let him get away with being right all the time. "I don't see what value there is in brown shoe polish taste."

"Be sensible, *Yew*gene. Smoking's got to have some value or everybody wouldn't do it, would they? You gotta admit that. What's the value, then, if it ain't that brown shoe polish taste?"

"When was the last time you polished your shoes, much less ate any brown shoe polish, Hawkins?"

"You forget, Richards, when I was little somebody got my dad a job as a shoe shine boy for a while, until he found some excuse to get out of it. He used to take me along sometimes because he figured I looked cute and would attract customers. I wasn't more than four, and I ate some shoe polish. I figured it would taste like chocolate."

"It must have jolted you some when you got it in your mouth."

"Funny thing was, I kind of liked it. I wasn't but four, remember. Finally Dad caught me at it. He said shoe polish was expensive. He couldn't afford to let me eat any of it, for it took all the profit out of the business."

We stopped joking around there. The cloud of Sonny's dad was suddenly hanging over us. I figured we had to get into it sometime. "Sonny, how's your mom going to manage with your dad gone?"

"I don't know," he said. "He wasn't much use to us. Spent as much as he brought in, I reckon. What little we had to spend."

I turned my head to look at him. "You don't miss him?"

He looked back at me. "Well, how do you feel about your dad?"

That was a hard question to answer. I couldn't remember my dad. He was gone by the time I was two. Of course I'd asked Mom about him—what kind of guy was he, and such, but she didn't want to talk about him. "That's a subject better left alone, Gene," she'd say. I think Grampa would have told me, but he didn't want to go against Mom. So I'd dropped it. "I don't know anything about my dad, Sonny."

"Didn't you ask them?"

"They won't tell me. They don't want to talk

about it. So I can't say if I miss him because I don't know what to miss." That wasn't exactly true, however. I thought a lot about what it would be like to have a dad. Was that the same as missing him? "I can see where there might be some value in having a dad, though. Do things with you. But I have Grampa."

"Not the same as having a dad."

"I don't see what the difference is." This conversation was making me feel lonely.

"It ain't the same," he said loudly. I was surprised that he was getting sore about it. "It ain't the same. I'm telling you, Gene, it ain't the same." His fists were clenched and his eyelids were scrunched closed. "It ain't the same." Then he began to cry, sobbing away to beat the band, the tears running down his cheeks. He turned over on his face with his arms under his head and went on sobbing, his back going up and down until he was gasping for breath. He had a lot to cry about, I reckoned—his dad being dead, and not being much use when he'd been there.

I touched him on his back. "It's okay, Sonny."

"Go away," he said. "Just go away, Gene."

I stood and walked up the river a ways. But I didn't leave. Instead I crouched down there by the river, playing with a little stick in the dirt for a while, and then I went back to the willow tree.

He was sitting up against the tree trunk, staring at the river, his eyes red. "You okay?" I said.

"I guess so," he said. "I guess it's okay to cry when your dad dies, even if he wasn't much use."

"Sure it is," I said.

"I didn't think I was gonna blubber over it. It kind of took me by surprise."

"You weren't prepared for him to die. It would have been different if he'd been old and sick."

"No, we wasn't prepared for it."

I waited a minute and then my curiosity got too much for me. "What happened, exactly? Grampa said he might have jumped off that lumber platform."

Sonny shook his head hard. "He didn't. It wasn't like that at all. He didn't jump off there."

"He just missed his footing?"

Sonny didn't say anything for the longest

while, and I kept my mouth shut and waited. Then he said, "He was hearing a voice. You're not to tell anyone, Gene. Nobody knows it but me and Mom. The girls don't know; my aunt don't know."

"A voice?" I was getting the strangest feeling.

"He didn't like to talk about it, but it worried him a whole lot and sometimes it burst out of him."

"Where was the voice coming from?"

"Inside of him," he said. "Telling him to do things. He said he kept fighting the voice off, but it was a struggle."

I was scared to find out more, but I had to. "What was it saying?"

"Crazy stuff. Once it told him to dive in front of a car. Once it told him to drink iodine. He'd nicked himself with his fishing knife cleaning a fish and was putting iodine on the cut. Suddenly the voice told him to drink the iodine. He was struggling against it and somehow he dropped the bottle and the iodine spilled out."

"What happened when the voice told him to dive in front of the car?"

"He was all set to do it, he said. But luckily

the driver saw him leaning out into the road and hit his brakes. The driver told him afterwards he thought he was drunk. But he wasn't drunk. It was the voice. He said it was the hardest thing, fighting off that voice. He said he knew it was going to get him someday."

"Sonny, you think that voice told him to jump off the lumber platform?"

"I'll bet you dollars to doughnuts on it, Gene. That voice told him to walk out into midair, and he couldn't resist it no more. Out into midair he went."

Chapter 3

I couldn't sleep that night, but lay in bed staring at the streetlights flickering through the trees, thinking about it. I knew now that I wasn't just hearing things. Something was out there trying to get me. A spirit, specter — I didn't know what to call it. Whatever the name, it was real, for it had killed Mr. Hawkins.

It was after Grampa, that was certain — would like to kill him if it could. What about me? Would it try to get me to walk off some high place or dive in front of a car? The idea that this thing could get inside you and make you do things you never wanted to do scared the pants off me. I shuddered when I thought of it.

It was like having strange things growing out of your skin.

Why was it after Grampa? Everybody in Magnolia thought the world of Grampa. They remembered that he'd once been a judge and a state senator, of course, and respected him for that. But there was more to it: people around town knew that Grampa was always straight with you. No matter whether you were the biggest man in town or somebody like Mr. Hawkins who hadn't had two nickels to rub together, Grampa would treat you honestly.

And why Mr. Hawkins? What had he got to do with Grampa and me? I never saw that much of Mr. Hawkins, and never had much conversation with him when I did. Just "Hello, Mr. Hawkins, is Sonny around?" The truth is, Mr. Hawkins didn't much like to bother with kids. Sonny said that his dad used to take him fishing sometimes, but that was mostly when he'd borrowed a boat and needed Sonny to row. Sonny said that was all right, he didn't mind rowing; it was kind of nice being out on the river with his dad, just the two of them, no snotty little sisters tagging along. Kind of nice, Sonny said, even if his dad didn't have much to say but "Over to the left a little, Sonny," or "Hold still right here." His dad was a pretty good fisherman, Sonny said, and they usually went home with a nice mess of fish for supper. But that was about as far as Mr. Hawkins' interest in kids went. He hardly knew who I was. He wasn't connected to the specter through me or Grampa.

These questions were buzzing around in my head like a swarm of bees. I knew I'd go crazy if I didn't find some answers to them. I couldn't go on living like this. It was like wrestling a waterfall: there was nothing you could grasp on to. Maybe Mr. Hawkins had walked out into midair because he couldn't stand thinking about these things any longer. I could see how you could get to that point.

It was clear enough that I'd better talk to Sam. She was kind of pretty: dark brown hair, brown eyes. We were both born in Magnolia, had gone to school together the whole time, same class most years. I don't know as she was my best friend—Sonny was that—but she was my oldest friend. Grampa and Mr. Samuels were friends, too, although Grampa was a good deal older than Mr. Samuels. Belonged to the Lions Club, worked on charities together. Our families had been getting together since we were pups. There wasn't much Sam and I didn't know about each other.

What was I going to tell Sam? She'd want to know too much—ask a lot of questions. But I didn't see any other way to go. I lay there trying to think up some story to tell her she might believe. In a while I came up with one. I felt better after that and finally fell asleep.

I caught Sam after school the next day. "I've got to talk to you," I said.

"I can't. I have Girl Scouts."

"After Girl Scouts, then."

"I can't then, either. Mom's taking me to Weinberg's for a summer outfit."

"It's important, Sam. I have to talk to you."

"Tomorrow," she said. "I can do it tomorrow. I'll meet you at Hoags for sodas."

"No," I said. "It's private. Too many people there. Meet me at the bandstand. There won't be anybody around."

She wrinkled her forehead. "Why? What's the big secret about it?"

"I can't tell you now. I'll tell you tomorrow."

. . .

We had a little park in Magnolia on the riverbank—gravel paths, big elm trees with their branches hanging downwards, park benches. Cool and shady in the summer. In the middle there was a bandstand, just a round platform a couple of feet off the ground, with a roof over it to shade it from the sun. On Sunday afternoons in the summer the Volunteer Firemen's Band played there. The mayor made a speech from the bandstand on the Fourth of July with everybody waving little flags at him, and if the governor or some senator was in town, which wasn't often, they'd make their speeches from the bandstand. Sometimes on rainy days in the summer, kids would roller-skate on it, but it really was too small for that. Mostly the bandstand just sat there, waiting for somebody to come.

It was empty when I got there. In a couple of minutes Sam came up. She had an apple left over from her school lunch and we took turns taking bites out of it, each from our own side. "So what's the big secret, Gene?"

I was feeling pretty nervous, worried she'd find holes in my story. But I had to go ahead. "I heard something about my grampa," I said. "I'm worried about it."

She stared at me, her eyes bright. Having a mystery to chew on suited Sam right down to the ground. "Like what? Heard what?"

"I heard that back when we were little, Grampa did something really bad."

"Bad? What do you mean by that? Against the law?"

"I don't know what it was, just that it was very bad. It was back when we were maybe two years old or something. I figured there might be something in your dad's newspaper about it."

"I never heard of your grampa doing anything bad. Nobody did. Why do you believe it? Who told it to you?"

I took a deep breath. "Sonny Hawkins' dad told me."

"Sonny Hawkins' dad? The guy who killed

himself?" She went on staring at me, her eyes bright. This was getting pretty interesting to her.

"I don't think he killed himself. Sonny says he didn't. Sonny says he'd been having dizzy spells recently, and that's what happened. He was up there on the lumber platform and had a dizzy spell."

"Everybody says he killed himself. Just walked off into the air."

"Well, they're wrong. He didn't." I was getting stubborn about it. Funny as it seemed, Mr. Hawkins and I were together in the same thing. I was on his side about it. "People shouldn't say stuff like that when they don't know anything about it. He had a dizzy spell."

Sam shrugged. "The cops say they have eyewitness reports. There were four guys working right there, getting down those two-by-sixes, and they all saw him walk off into the air."

"Is your dad going to put that in the paper?"

"I don't know," she said. "He doesn't always put everything in the paper. He says if it's going to hurt a lot of people to no purpose he'll leave it out."

"Tell him this will hurt Sonny and Mrs. Hawkins and the girls," I said.

"There's no use in telling Dad anything when it comes to the *Chronicle*. He says he can't run the paper to suit his family. How come Mr. Hawkins decided to tell you this stuff about your grampa?"

I hadn't figured she'd ask that. "I don't know why he told me; he just did. I was out at Sonny's practicing double plays with a tennis ball when Mr. Hawkins came along. We got into a conversation and he said that Grampa had done something really bad back then." There wasn't much truth to any of that. For one thing, Mr. Hawkins never had much to say to Sonny, much less me. "It doesn't matter why he told me. He just did."

"Why do you believe him?" she said. "Mr. Hawkins is known for being bone lazy."

"What has being lazy got to do with telling lies?"

"A lot. If he won't do an honest day's work, why would he be honest about the truth?"

"Do you have to argue about everything, Sam?" I was getting exasperated. "You're always grilling me. What he told me was what he told me."

She looked down. "I'm sorry, Gene. I didn't mean to grill you. But the whole thing seems sort of weird."

Of course she was right. I wasn't used to lying to Sam, and I could see that I hadn't done a good job of it. It embarrassed me. I had figured that I could say I'd got this stuff about Grampa from Mr. Hawkins because he was dead and couldn't deny it; I had forgot that it wasn't very realistic for Mr. Hawkins to have told me anything like that. "Let's get off Sonny's dad. The main thing is whether I could look through back issues of the *Chronicle* to see if there's anything about Grampa in it."

"Dad's got all the back issues on shelves in the storage room behind his office. They go way back to before Dad bought the paper, back into the 1890s or something. Dad won't let anybody look through the real old issues unless they've got a good reason. They're kind of yellow and crumbly."

"I don't think this goes back that far. Just back to when we were little."

"Then that's probably okay," Sam said. "He'd probably let us look at those."

Us. I should have known that if there was a mystery involved Sam would have to get in on it. "Maybe you wouldn't want to waste your time on it."

"Oh, it'll be fun. I like reading the old papers. Seeing the funny clothes the ladies wore, the old-fashioned cars."

I wouldn't be able to talk her out of it. So we made our plan. We'd tell Sam's dad that we were working on a school project together—we'd done that before. We'd meet Saturday morning at the *Chronicle* office.

When I got home that afternoon Grampa was reading the *Chronicle*. "Delivering groceries, Gene?" he asked.

I blushed and for a minute I thought of lying about it. But I wasn't much of a liar. "I was playing baseball."

He didn't say anything, but I knew he was disappointed in me. Grampa didn't expect me to give up playing baseball altogether, but I knew I ought to go to Snuffy's more regularly than I had been doing recently.

Grampa shook the paper. "There's a story here about Sonny's dad." He folded the paper to the story and handed it to me. It was on page three, kind of short.

Unexplained Death of Magnolia Man
A local man, Frank Hawkins, plunged to his death Monday from the second-tier platform at Magnolia Hardware and Lumber. According to witnesses, Hawkins appeared to deliberately step off the platform. He was pronounced dead at Hardscrabble County Hospital. Witnesses said that Hawkins might have survived the fall, but that some of the lumber he had been handling followed him down, breaking his back and injuring his skull.

The story went on from there to say Mr. Hawkins had lived on River Road, and was survived by his wife, and so forth.

"Grampa, are they saying that Mr. Hawkins jumped off on purpose?"

"That's the idea, I guess. They were all

talking about it at the garage when I went in to have the oil changed on the Model A. Billy Tolliver said he heard that Hawkins had been drinking."

I was bound and determined to stay on Mr. Hawkins' side. "I never saw Mr. Hawkins drunk. I've been around their place more than anyone. He didn't drink much."

"I didn't think he did," Grampa said. "I never heard of it, anyway. But all the fellows at the lumberyard swear he walked off that platform."

I knew better. "Why would somebody decide to kill himself in the middle of the morning for no good reason?"

Grampa shook his head. "You never know about these things, Gene. He might have been brooding about it for days—for weeks, maybe. Been thinking about it since he got up that morning and all at once he got tired of having it buzzing around in his mind and jumped."

Buzzing around in his mind—just like me. I didn't like that idea very much. "Why would somebody jump when he was only fifteen feet up? He might have only busted a leg. He couldn't count on that lumber following him down."

"Yes, that's true, Gene. But I don't imagine that a fellow in that state of mind would be thinking very clearly about things."

I didn't like Mr. Hawkins being blamed for his own death. "Grampa, it isn't fair for everybody to be saying that Mr. Hawkins killed himself when he's dead and can't defend himself."

Grampa nodded. "That's true, Gene. You're right. We shouldn't form hasty conclusions. I get your point. It's especially unfair to Sonny and his family." He stopped to think. "Perhaps I could write a letter to the *Chronicle*." He considered some more. "Or perhaps you could. That's a better idea."

"Me?" That was pretty startling.

"Sure. Why not? You're closer to the Hawkins family than anyone else. You have strong feelings about what's going on. Just write exactly what you've been telling me. Put down your feelings about it."

The whole idea made me uncomfortable. I was just some kid. I wasn't important enough to write a letter to the paper. Sam, she'd have done it in a shot. If she had an opinion about something, which mostly she did, she'd let you know.

But that was Sam, not me. "They wouldn't print a letter by some kid."

"Why not?" Grampa said. "I think Al Samuels would find it interesting to run a letter expressing the viewpoint of a youngster. It's a different approach. Newspapers like to find unusual things to run."

Suddenly it occurred to me that the specter might not like it if I were to write such a letter. It seemed clear enough that it wouldn't want people saying nice things about Mr. Hawkins. I sure didn't want to bring the specter down on me any more than necessary. "I'm not a very good writer," I said. "Just average."

"Most people aren't expert writers," Grampa said. "You write well enough for this. Just put on paper what you've been telling me. I'll take the letter to Al Samuels myself."

As usual, what Grampa said made sense, but of course he didn't know the truth of it—the specter and all that. On top of it, I'd never wanted to be anybody special. I just wanted to be a plain kid. "Grampa, I'd better ask Sonny first. He might not like it. He might want everybody to shut up about it."

Grampa nodded. "Possibly. Ask Sonny, then."

The next day after school I went to Snuffy's to see if there were any deliveries. There were a couple—a big box for old Mr. and Mrs. Tonelli, who hardly had any money at all and would tip me only a nickel, and a box for Mrs. Frye, who was usually good for a dime. So I made the deliveries, which made me feel a little better about myself, and then I went over to Sonny's. It was a pretty nice day, just right for baseball, so we went to the flat, grassy place between his house and the river and threw grounders and pop flies to each other.

I wasn't sure how to bring the subject up—plain didn't want to, in fact. But I'd promised Grampa, and I had to do it. So finally, after we'd been tossing the ball around for twenty minutes, I stood there, dropping the ball into my glove and taking it out again. "Sonny, did you see the story in the *Chronicle* about your dad?"

"No," he said. "I never read it. Dad said most of what you read in the newspapers was a bunch of lies."

"It said that your dad walked off that lumber platform on purpose."

"He didn't. I know it. That voice told him to do it and he couldn't hold himself back."

"I don't misbelieve that," I said. "I believe it's true. But people are saying he did it on purpose."

He slammed his right fist into his fielder's glove. "It isn't true!" he shouted. "He didn't. They shouldn't say that."

"Grampa said I should write a letter to the paper about it. You know, say it isn't fair to gossip about somebody when they aren't there to defend themselves."

He stopped slamming his fist into his glove and stared at me. "They wouldn't put it in the paper," he said finally.

"Grampa said they might. He says he would carry the letter over to Mr. Samuels himself."

Sonny went on staring at me. "Your grampa said that?"

"He said he would."

He looked at me for a while longer. Then he spit into the grass. "Naw, they wouldn't put nothing good about us in the paper."

"Grampa says they would."

"I don't believe it. Dad always said that

nobody gives a plugged nickel about you if you don't have the bucks. Not around here, anyways."

Now, if I left it at that I could get out of it. Just tell Grampa that Sonny wasn't in favor of the letter. But I knew that wasn't exactly the truth. "Sonny, I could try," I said, hoping he'd say to forget it.

But he didn't. He stared at me for the longest time. Then he said, "Would you do it, Gene?"

I didn't want to, that was for sure. "Sure I would, Sonny."

"I'd sure appreciate it."

I figured the sooner I got it over with, the better, so I said I'd do it right then, and I went home. Nobody was there. I went up to my room, tore a piece of paper out of my notebook, and spent a while sharpening a pencil, still trying to think of a way to get out of it. But there wasn't any.

How did you begin? Dear *Magnolia Chronicle*? Dear Editor? Dear Mr. Samuels? I decided I'd leave room for that and ask Grampa about it later. What next? I chewed on my pencil for a while. Then I wrote, "It isn't fair for—" I stopped. Fair for what? I tried again. "It said in the paper that—" But I couldn't remember exactly what it had said in the paper. I tried again. "People shouldn't gossip about Mr. Hawkins when—"

Then I felt that familiar tightness come into my chest, that pressure, and things slowly started moving around inside of me. "Please leave me alone," I said. "Please go away."

"I'm not happy about this letter, Gene. I'd rather you drop it."

"Why are you bothering me?"

"Let's not go through all that again. It's the letter that concerns me."

"If I forget about the letter, will you leave me alone?"

"I'm afraid we've still got some tasks to do before that happens, Gene. For the moment I want you to forget about the letter."

"There must be some way to get rid of you!" I shouted.

The specter chuckled. "But I'm not very likely to tell you, am I?"

I thought: there might be some hope in that. "Why did you have to kill Mr. Hawkins?"

"He deserved it, Gene. He did something very naughty back then. He deserved what he got."

"Back at the same time as Grampa did his bad thing?"

"Smart lad," the specter said. "They were all involved. When you and your little girlfriend start looking into it, you'll see how it ties together. Now just put away your pencil and paper."

"You can't make me," I said.

"Oh, you think not?" It gave that rusty chuckle, like sandpaper on metal. "Wait and see." The pressure in my chest began to loosen, the movement in my guts slowed, and then it was gone.

I sat there feeling sad and shaken. Could the voice really prevent me from writing that letter? I had a feeling that it could, but I couldn't see how. I had to try. I couldn't forgive myself if I didn't, and neither would Sonny.

I picked up the pencil and looked at the paper where I had scrawled the words "People shouldn't gossip about Mr. Hawkins when—" It seemed easy enough. All I needed to do was finish with "he isn't here to defend himself. We shouldn't jump to conclusions. We should give everybody the benefit of the doubt." That would be enough. Then sign my name, give it to Grampa, and the whole thing was done.

So I raised the pencil and leaned forward, and just then a new thought came into my mind: why should I have to write a letter just to please Grampa and Sonny? Was it *my* responsibility? Who said it was? I leaned back in my chair and stared up at the ceiling, my hand with the pencil in it dangling by my side. Now that I thought about it, the whole thing was making me kind of sore. What difference did it make to me that Sonny's dad had walked off that lumber platform into midair? Mr. Hawkins wasn't any friend of mine. When you got down to it, he'd hardly ever even taken the trouble to talk to me. Never gave me a stick of gum, had a catch with me, or took me out fishing with him. Why did I give a hoot about him?

Or Sonny and Grampa for that matter. Why was I supposed to help out Sonny just because we played baseball together? I played baseball with a lot of kids. Was I supposed to write letters for all of them? The more I thought about it, the sorer I got. The heck with them all. I wasn't going to waste my time feeling sorry for them. I threw the pencil onto my desk, crumpled up the piece of paper I'd been writing on, and tossed it toward my wastebasket. It bounced off the side of the basket and fell onto the floor. I let it lie there, and went downstairs to see if Grampa or Mom had come home yet.

And I probably wouldn't have thought of that letter again for a while, except that as I was clearing the dishes off the table after supper, Grampa said, "How are you coming along with that letter for the *Chronicle*, Gene? I ran into Al Samuels this afternoon and told him about it. He said he'd be interested to see it."

All at once I felt mighty ashamed of myself. I saw that the specter had beaten me after all. It couldn't actually force the pencil out of my hand, or rip up the paper I was writing on — it didn't have the power to do that. But somehow it had twisted my thoughts around and stirred up a lot of feelings that weren't normal to me. I felt awful to think that the specter could rummage around in my head like that, adding and subtracting whatever it wanted. It made me feel like I didn't belong to myself anymore. What else could it make me think?

But I had to tell Grampa something. "I'm having a hard time figuring out what to say, Grampa."

"Keep trying, Gene," he said. "It's a chance for you to show your respect for Sonny."

But I knew now that I'd never be able to write that letter.

Chapter 4

On Saturday morning I met Sam at the offices of the *Magnolia Chronicle*. The skies had clouded over; there would be rain. Mr. Samuels was at his desk, hammering at his typewriter. He looked around when I came in. "Alice is in the back room, Gene," he said. Then he went back to hammering.

I went out into the storeroom. There were a lot of plain pine shelves around the walls holding boxes of typing paper, envelopes, packets of rubber bands, jars of rubber cement. The stacks of old *Chronicles* took up one wall and gave off an old, damp smell.

Sam was already reading a paper. "You're late," she said.

"Come on, five minutes late."

"Late is late."

"I suppose you were never late. I see you come rushing into school with your hair flying and your shirt untucked just before the bell half the time."

"Not half the time. Every once in a while," she said.

I decided to change the topic. "What year are you reading?"

"You said it was when we were little."

"I don't know for sure exactly. Mr. Hawkins said it was around that time. It could have been a couple of years earlier or later."

"Well, I'm starting with 1923," Sam said. "Then we can branch out."

So we divided up the papers for 1923, and sat on the floor with our legs crossed and began turning the pages. "What exactly do you think we're looking for, Gene?"

"Anything about my grampa. Judge John Wesley Adamson."

"I never knew he had such a fancy name," Sam said.

"Remember, he was a state senator and a

judge back then. It helps to have a fancy name to get those kinds of jobs."

"You mean if your name was Joe Snooze you couldn't be a judge?"

"How could you? Who'd pay attention to a guy called Judge Snooze?"

She giggled. "Dad says most of the judges have been asleep for years anyway."

"Hey, this is serious. Let's cut out the chitchat."

We were quiet for a bit, turning pages and reading. It was slow going, for your eye was always catching some interesting little story — a pig got into the Baptist church during morning services and raced squealing around the pews with the deacon after him with a broom; lightning struck Elmer's corn silo and knocked out the hired man who was down below forking out silage; some old woman who remembered back when there were still Indians around Magnolia had a hundredth birthday party; new law setting a ten-mile-an-hour speed limit downtown. Not much real excitement to it, but it was different, and we kept stopping to read out loud to each other.

It took us more than an hour to get through 1923. We decided to make a rule against reading things out loud to each other, unless it was *really* interesting — no more pigs in churches and hired men hit by lightning. We started off on 1924. The trouble was deciding what counted as really interesting and qualified to be read out loud, and what was just plain interesting and didn't. Generally, by the time one of us had decided, we were already reading it out loud and it was too late. So by noon we'd gotten through only two years and a bit of a third one and had to quit. Sam had to go to a birthday party that afternoon and I'd promised myself I'd go to Snuffy's to see if there were any deliveries. We agreed to come back Sunday after church. Grampa wasn't big on church and didn't care if I went, but Mom went a lot and was likely to make me go if I couldn't find a way to wriggle out of it. The *Chronicle* office would be closed on Sunday, but Sam said she could get a key from her dad.

So I went home for lunch — heated up macaroni and cheese with some leftover ham and peas stirred into it. We ate, chatting about this and that. Then, as we were almost finished eating and I was about to excuse myself, Grampa reached into his shirt pocket and pulled out a piece of paper. It was wrinkled, but Grampa had smoothed it out. I knew right away what it was: the letter I'd started writing to the *Chronicle* about Sonny's dad.

Grampa laid it on the table facing me. There were the words I'd written: "People shouldn't gossip about Mr. Hawkins." "Gene, I went up to your room to collect your dirty laundry for your mom and I picked this up off the floor. I was going to throw it away when I realized what it was."

I bent my head forward and looked down at my plate. Of course it hadn't been my fault, really; it had been the specter's fault. But it felt like I had done something bad all the same. I took a quick glance at Mom out of the corner of my eye.

She was looking puzzled. "What's this about?"

I raised my head. I couldn't think of what to say. "It's hard to explain," I said.

Mom wrinkled her forehead. "What's hard to explain? There's something going on around here that I'm not getting."

Grampa spoke to Mom, but he looked at me. "Gene's the one who can explain it."

What was I going to do? Burst out shouting that I was being haunted by a specter that wouldn't let me write that letter? They'd think I was crazy and take me to a nut doctor. "I was trying to see what to say in case I was going to write it." It sounded pretty feeble even to me.

Mom was still looking puzzled. "I demand to know what this is about."

"It's no secret," Grampa said. "Gene didn't think people should be gossiping about Frank Hawkins. They shouldn't be saying he jumped off that lumber platform when there isn't enough evidence for it. Gene's sure it was an accident."

It wasn't an accident: Mr. Hawkins was murdered. But I couldn't tell them that. "He was having dizzy spells. Sonny said so."

"If that's the case, then write to the *Chronicle* about it," Grampa said.

"I don't know what the fuss is about," Mom said.

I looked away from them out the window. We had a big maple tree in our front yard with a tire swing hanging from a big branch. Grampa had put it up for me when we moved here. He used to swing me on the tire swing when I was too little to swing myself, going way up until I was high above the world. I wished I was a little kid again, swinging on that tire swing, with nothing to worry about but seeing how high I could go. "I don't think Sonny wants me to write any letter. He doesn't like to talk about it." I wondered how many lies my soul could take before it broke down.

Grampa nodded. "Well, that's understand-able."

"Yes," Mom said. "I don't imagine it's a pleasant subject for him."

I looked from one of them to the other. "Still, Mr. Hawkins didn't jump off there."

"How do you know that, Gene?" Mom said. "You weren't there."

I went on looking them in the eye, one after another. "I just know, is all." Mom and Grampa were looking at each other, and I knew they were deciding to drop it.

. . .

On Sunday morning I went over to the *Chronicle* office. Sam wasn't there yet, so I sat on the steps and waited. In a couple of minutes she came rushing up, her hair flying, tucking in her shirt. "So who's late now?" I said.

"I couldn't help it. Mom made me change out of my church clothes before I could go out." Sam took the office key out of her skirt pocket. We went in, sat cross-legged on the floor, and started amid the smell of dust and old papers. We were working on the spring of 1925 when I hit on a story that caught my eye. There wasn't much to it. The headline said *Old Toffey Farm to Be Sold*. The story said:

> The two-hundred-acre farm formerly belonging to the late William Toffey, whose family had occupied the farm for four generations, is under option for sale to Mr. Ernest Gallen of Chicago. Mr. Toffey's great-grandfather, Albro Toffey, was one of the earliest settlers of Hardscrabble County, and later a figure in state politics. Mr. Toffey's widow, Alma Toffey, says, "I hate to sell the old place, but it's too much for me to keep up anymore."

Mr. Gallen says he is buying the place for "investment purposes."

The reason why the story caught my eye was because back when I was a little kid Mom and I used to go up to the old Toffey place berry picking. The Toffeys had been important people around Magnolia once. There was a Toffey Street in town and a Toffey Building downtown. I didn't know much about it, but obviously the Toffeys had come down in the world from what they'd once been. The old Toffey house was a half mile down at the end of the road from the old house where we used to live, Grampa's big house with white columns out front and the gravel driveway circling up to it. By the time I was four or five years old, big enough for berry picking, the Toffey house was standing empty. The fields were growing up to brush—small cedars, briars, saplings coming into the fields where cows had grazed and corn had once grown. But the berries were plentiful, if you got there ahead of the birds. Like most farmers, the Toffeys had put in blue-berries and raspberries, which didn't need much taking care of. Wild blackcaps had come in, too.

So Mom and I would go down the road — dirt road then — to the Toffey house with our buckets and fill them up with enough berries for a couple of pies. Blueberry pie with ice cream — about the best eating there was in the world, I figured back then. Oh, I liked going down there with Mom. Mighty pleasant with the sun on my back, picking berries and eating a good few of them, too, when Mom wasn't looking.

But the old Toffey house took some of the fun out of it. Some of the windows were broken, the porch roof hung down at one end, the main roof sagged, the chimneys tilted. That forlorn old house scared me. Those dark, empty windows seemed like the eyes of an evil cat staring at us, just watching, always watching, waiting to pounce. Generally I managed to keep my eyes on the berry bushes and didn't think about the house. But I couldn't help glancing at it now and again. When I did, it gave me the shivers. Of course I was pretty little then.

So that's why I was pulled into that story. I hadn't laid eyes on that old Toffey house since we'd moved away from there after the hard times came in 1930. Was it still standing? A lot of time these old abandoned houses burned down. Hoboes camping would set them afire by accident. Or somebody would burn one on purpose, just to watch the flames roaring and hear the fire trucks come rumbling up, their sirens wailing. So maybe it was gone. I didn't know.

"Listen to this, Sam," I said. I read it out to her.

"I don't see what's so interesting about that."

She was right. "It's interesting to me. I used to pick berries up there with my mom when I was a little kid. I was scared of that old house."

"Oh," she said. "I can see where it might be interesting to you, but it isn't to anyone else."

"Why did your dad put it in the paper, then, if it wasn't interesting?" I said.

She frowned. She didn't want to hear that her dad had made a mistake about what he'd put in the newspaper. "It might have been interesting to people back then."

"Yes, but what was interesting about it?"

She reached over from where she was sitting, took the newspaper from me, and read the story. "Oh, sure, Gene," she said. "This guy Gallen was going to use the place for investment purposes. There might be money in it. That was what was interesting about it."

We sat and considered it. "Maybe," I said, "Grampa was going to invest in it, or something, seeing as it was a half mile down the road from his house."

"Let's keep an eye out," Sam said. "It might lead us somewhere."

We went on turning pages. From time to time we spotted a story about Grampa. *Judge Adamson to Speak at Kiwanis Club*. Or a picture of Grampa and some other high muckety-mucks in the lobby of the Magnolia Hotel. But by noon we'd found nothing of importance. Sam looked at her watch. "I have to go home for lunch."

"I better go, too." So we put the newspapers back where they belonged, and left. Sam locked the door. "We aren't getting anywhere, Gene," she said. "It's getting kind of boring."

"Well, if you want to quit, okay. I know there was something going on back then. Something serious."

"How do you know?"

I was tempted to tell her. Carrying a thing

like that around weighs you down. It would have been a relief to talk to somebody about it. But I'd decided against it. She'd ask a whole lot of questions. Knowing Sam, she would want to hear the voice herself. Or at least hear me talking to it. "Just from what Mr. Hawkins told me. He said that a man got killed out of it."

"Are you saying there was a murder? Dad would have known about that. It's bound to be in the paper." Her eyes were shining. "Well, if there was a murder I guess we ought to keep going." That was Sam: set a mystery in front of her and she couldn't resist.

When I got home Mom was putting out bologna sandwiches and Grampa was reading the Sunday paper from St. Louis. "How'd the Cards do yesterday?" I asked.

"Not so good. The Pirates creamed them." He laid the paper in his lap. "Sonny Hawkins stopped by a little while ago. He wanted to see you. He wanted to know if you'd written that letter. He said it was mighty kind of me to take it over to the *Chronicle*." Grampa looked at me for a minute. "What's this all about, Gene?"

It was getting to be too much for me. "I can't

tell you," I said. Mom had stopped what she was doing and had started listening.

"You can't tell us?" Grampa was pretty surprised. "What's so bad that you can't tell us?"

"I just can't tell you," I said.

"Gene," Mom said, "you can always tell—"

"No!" I shouted, waving my hands. "No, no."

"Gene," Grampa said. "You'll have to tell Sonny something."

It all came boiling out of me. "Just leave me alone, leave me alone." I started to cry, so I flung my arm over my eyes and ran upstairs.

"Gene—" Mom said.

"Leave him alone for a bit, May," Grampa said.

I ran into my room and slammed the door.

Chapter 5

I lay on my bed looking at the ceiling, wiping my eyes and trying not to think of anything. I hadn't been lying there for five minutes when I felt the voice moving around inside me like a little animal. "No!" I shouted. "Not you, either." I began to drum on my stomach with both hands.

"Well," said the hollow voice, "we certainly are in a bad mood today, aren't we."

"Shut up!" I shouted. "I hate you."

"Come, come, Gene. That's a very unpleasant thing to say. We should love our fellow creatures."

I realized that if I kept shouting, Grampa and Mom would hear it and come up. "I'll never love you," I said, keeping my voice low. "Never."

"Oh, you might, Gene, you might. Never say never."

I didn't say anything for a minute. Then I said, "What do you want?"

"That letter. I told you I didn't want it written, but you ignored me, and now it's gotten you into a lot of trouble."

"I didn't write it," I said. "You know that."

"But you started to. You should have listened to me in the first place."

I was quiet. Then I said, "Is that all you want, just to gloat at me because I got in trouble with Mom and Grampa?"

"I'm not gloating, Gene. I'm simply trying to make the point that I often know what's best for you. You must learn to trust me more."

"Trust you?" I said, still trying to keep my voice low. "Trust you? When you've done nothing but wreck my life? Why should I trust you?"

Then I heard Mom's footsteps on the stairs. In a moment the door to my room opened and Mom came in. "I brought you a sandwich and some milk," she said.

The hollow voice said, "We'll discuss this

sometime when you're in a better mood." It disappeared.

I sat up on my bed with my feet on the floor. "I'll come down and have lunch." I felt calmer.

"All right," she said. She paused for a minute. "Who were you talking to just a moment ago?"

I was pretty calm now. "Nobody. I was only talking to myself."

"It sounded as if you were having an argument with somebody."

"I was arguing with myself. Let's not talk about it, Mom. I'll come down and have lunch."

But I knew I'd have to talk to Sonny, so after lunch I set off for his place. He was out in the dirt yard, bouncing a tennis ball off the side of the house to practice his fielding. "Where'd you get the tennis ball?"

"Over at the country club," he said.

"Where was the ball?"

"Laying in the grass beside the courts."

"You're going to get caught doing that someday," I said. "Around the sixth time you tell them you're looking for a job they might admire your persistence and give you one."

"Naw," Sonny said. "I'll tell 'em I'm allergic."

"Allergic to what?"

"Whatever the job is. If it's mowing the lawn I'll say I'm allergic to grass. If it's washing dishes in the clubhouse, I'm allergic to dishwashing soap. You can always get out of anything if you say you're allergic."

"You can't get out of homework by saying you're allergic," I said. "They'll give you an F anyway."

"Sure you can. You can say you're allergic to pencil lead."

"They'll tell you to write with a pen," I said.

"Maybe I'll tell them I'm allergic to F's." He shook his head and shoved the tennis ball in his pants pocket. "I'm tired of this. Let's go down to the river and see if there's anything floating by."

So we went down to the river and lay in the shade of the big willow tree, with our backs against the trunk, enjoying the river smells and the breeze coming through the willow leaves. But I wasn't totally comfortable, because I knew I had to talk about that letter. "The Cards didn't do so hot yesterday," I said.

"I didn't see the paper," Sonny said. "What happened?"

Sonny's dad had always said that everything in the paper was a bunch of lies and wouldn't waste his money on it. They got their news from the radio, the problem being that Sonny's mom mostly had the radio tuned to soap operas, except when the snotty little girls wanted to listen to *Little Orphan Annie* or *Tom Mix*. Sonny generally found out about the Cardinals a day late when he came across yesterday's newspaper in a garbage can. "They got creamed."

"Where'd you get that?"

"From Grampa. He gets the paper as soon as it comes out in the morning."

Sonny gave me a sideways look. "I stopped by your house this morning to see if you wanted to go over to the country club with me to hook tennis balls."

That left it up to me. I didn't like it any, but there was no way around it. "Grampa told me. He said you asked him about that letter I was supposed to write to the paper."

"Yeah. What ever became of that?"

"I couldn't write it, Sonny."

He was chewing on a piece of grass and looking at me, his back still up against the trunk of the tree. "How come you couldn't write it? You don't have no trouble zooming along on that stuff they make us write for school."

"Yeah, I know, but that isn't real; it's just school. This was real. I started it, but I just couldn't do it. I really tried, but the words wouldn't come out." It sounded kind of flat, like I hadn't tried very hard. I wished now that I'd given a little more thought to what to tell Sonny. I should have made up some reasonable excuse, like Grampa having asked Mr. Samuels about it, and Mr. Samuels saying he didn't want to put it in the paper. It just seemed like everywhere I turned these days I had to tell some lie.

Sonny went on looking at me and chewing on the grass. "Why wouldn't the words come out? All you gotta do is tell people to shut up about my dad jumping off that lumber platform. That's all. Just tell 'em that."

"I know that, Sonny. I know what to say. I just couldn't get myself to do it."

He looked puzzled. "What do you mean, you couldn't get yourself to do it?"

I hadn't expected him to argue about it. I could see now how much it meant to him. Bad enough that his dad was kind of a no-good. "Maybe I could try again," I said. That was just to stop him from arguing about it; I knew it wouldn't work.

He flung the chewed grass away and frowned down at the ground. "I don't get how you couldn't make yourself do it, *Yew*gene."

"I just couldn't."

"Why couldn't you?"

I was beginning to lose my temper. "I just couldn't. Why can't you leave it alone, Sonny?"

"Because you promised, *Yew*gene."

"Okay!" I shouted. "I promised. I couldn't do it."

"That isn't much of a promise."

I knelt away from the willow trunk. "All right, I'll tell you why, Sonny!" I shouted. "You know that voice your dad was hearing? It's inside me, too."

He knelt and stared at me. "You got that voice, too, Gene?" he said in a wondering tone.

"Yes, I have." I was feeling pretty shaky, which surprised me, because I hadn't realized how worked up I was. But it was a relief to have gotten it out to somebody, instead of carrying it around all by myself. "It came on last week out of the blue. I don't know why it picked me out. Something to do with Grampa—it said he'd done something real bad a while back. It won't tell me what—said I had to find out for myself, otherwise I wouldn't believe it. I hate it, Sonny. But I can't stop it."

Sonny went on staring at me, like I had suddenly turned into a troll or a witch or something. "That's what Dad said. He begged the voice to go away and leave him alone, but it wouldn't. There was no way to stop it."

"Did your dad say it was there all the time, or came and went?"

He was still staring at me like I'd become a magical creature. "Came and went," Sonny said. "Leave him alone for two or three days so's Dad would think it'd gone for good; and then here it comes again."

"Just like me. I wish I'd known your dad was having the voice, too. I would have felt a lot better talking to somebody about it. Maybe we could have figured out what to do." For the first time in my life I felt kind of friendly toward Sonny's dad.

Sonny plucked another piece of grass and began chewing on it. "Does the voice tell you to do dangerous things—dive in front of a car or jump out a window?"

We were still both kneeling, facing each other. "No. Nothing dangerous. I don't think it's trying to get me the way it was trying to get your dad."

"That's different, then. The voice was out to get my dad, and finally it did." He didn't say anything for a minute. Then he said, "You want to know the truth, Gene? I'm blame glad I found this out. To be honest, I wasn't always sure myself that Dad was telling the truth about it. It was hard to believe he was hearing a voice. Sometimes I figured he must be nuts. But then I'd realize that there wasn't anything nuts about him in any other way. Same old person he always was. Not much use to us, but no different from how he'd been before. I couldn't decide one way or the other. It's kind of a relief to find out you got the voice, too."

"Not to me it isn't, Sonny."

"No, no, Gene," he said. "I wouldn't wish it

on you. I wouldn't wish it on anyone. But I'm glad to find out." He gave me a glance. "At least the voice isn't out to get you."

"At least that," I said. "It wants me to get Grampa. I figure the voice can't actually do anything itself. It has to get people to do things for it. Like that letter I was supposed to write for you—it couldn't stop me from doing it, but it could make me not want to write it."

"It can make you want to do bad things?"

"I think so. I think that's the size of it."

Sonny didn't say anything for a while, and I know he was thinking about his dad walking off that lumber platform into midair. "What are you going to do, Gene?"

"I don't know. I wish I did. The only thing I can think of is to find out what Grampa did that was supposed to be so bad."

We decided to quit talking about the voice. We played catch for a while and then I went on home. Anyway, it was a relief to have somebody to talk with. It wasn't going to put an end to it, but it helped some.

. . .

On Monday after school Sam and I went over to the *Chronicle* office to have another whack at those newspapers. I could have done it by myself, but it went twice as fast with two of us. Anyway, I was glad to have the company. For that matter, Sam wasn't going to be left out. Her curiosity wouldn't let her.

We were going along toward the middle of 1925 when Sam said, "Here's something about that old Toffey house where you used to pick blueberries."

"And raspberries. They weren't as good as blueberries for pie, but they were mighty good in a bowl with cream. What's the story say?"

"Not much." She handed me the paper.

Oil in Hardscrabble County?

The historic Toffey farm, one of the oldest farmhouses still standing in Hardscrabble County, may have oil deposits underneath it. At least that is the opinion of oil geologists, according to Mr. Ernest Gallen, who recently purchased the two-hundred-acre Toffey property. Says Gallen,

"Geologists from the Oil Institute of America whom I have consulted say that there are undoubtedly substantial oil deposits in the region west of St. Louis. The composition of the geological strata here is similar to that of the Oklahoma oil field to the southwest." Gallen says that a report on the potential for oil on the Toffey property is being prepared. He adds that several well-known figures, whom he cannot name at this time, are interested in developing this promising oil field.

That was all. "Nobody ever found oil out there so far as I know," I said. "I was berrying up there until I was seven years old, when the Depression hit and we had to move. I never saw anything up there but berry bushes and that old house staring at me with its dark, empty eyes."

"If there'd been oil around here we'd all be rich," Sam said. "Nobody's rich in Magnolia."

I handed her back the paper, and we went on

turning pages amid that musty paper smell. Then I hit another one that stopped me.

Oil Under Toffey Farm, Investor Says
There are likely to be deposits of oil under the historic Toffey farm, recently bought by Mr. Ernest Gallen of Chicago. According to Gallen, preliminary reports of an investigation made for him by geologists with the Oil Institute of America indicate that there may be a substantial amount of oil in the ground beneath the Toffey farm and the surrounding area. Gallen says that he intends to make the report available to the public when it is completed. When that will be Gallen was not sure. "We have got to be confident that we have our facts buttoned down before we issue the report," he said.

There was some stuff about the history of the old farm—how one of the Toffeys had got scalped by Indians a hundred years ago or something. That was all.

"What's this got to do with your grampa?" Sam asked.

"I don't know," I said. "I just have a feeling that it does. I can't tell you why."

"I think you're wasting your time over it. Let's forget about it. I want to find out what your grampa did that was so bad."

Once again we began turning pages. We didn't find anything. It was getting on toward suppertime, and we were getting bored with the whole thing. There weren't even any stories about pigs loose in church or farmers hit by lightning—just school board meetings and stores going out of business, which was pretty common since hard times came. "Let's quit," Sam said.

"Okay," I said. "Let me finish this last paper." I turned the page and there was another story about the old Toffey place. I took a quick look at it, and then I stopped. "Sam," I said. My skin felt prickly and my heart began to gallop.

"What?"

I felt strange, as if I'd been shifted out of myself and into somebody else. My heart was plowing along, and I was feeling cold. "Listen. The Toffey farm again." I began to read. "'Ernest Gallen, who is attempting to develop oil resources under the historic Toffey farm, which he recently purchased, has announced that he has taken a partner in the venture. He is a local man, Mr. Thomas Richards. Mr. Richards is married to the daughter of Judge John Wesley Adamson, a prominent figure in this area.'"

"Thomas Richards?" Sam said.

I shook myself to get off the chill. "That's my dad."

Chapter 6

Sam stared at me. "Are you sure it's your dad, Gene?"

"Thomas Richards. Tommy, everybody called him. How many Tommy Richards could there be around here? Besides, it said he was married to Judge Adamson's daughter. That's Mom."

She thought about it for a minute, trying to find another explanation. "Well, maybe your grampa had another daughter. This guy would be your uncle."

"Come on, Sam. Grampa had two daughters and they both married guys named Thomas Richards? Don't be so suspicious all the time."

"I'm not being suspicious, blame you, Gene.

I just want to be sure of the facts. You never talk about your dad. How am I supposed to know?"

It was true: I never talked much about him. There wasn't much for me to say, for I could hardly remember him. He left when I was around two. But I thought about him sometimes. Maybe more than just sometimes. Wondered where he was, what he was doing. What did he look like? Was he tall, good-looking, have a mustache? What kind of person was he? Jolly, talkative, liked to tell jokes? Or more the quiet type who didn't say much, but was likely to be right when he did say something? Sometimes in my imagination I'd be sitting at home by myself, and there'd come a knock at the door. I'd go to see who it was. There'd be a man standing there — tall, dressed in a fine suit, and behind him, parked on the street, a big Cadillac. "Hello," he'd say. "You must be Eugene. I'm your dad. Come on, I'll take you for a ride in my Caddy."

Or a letter would come in the mail for me, saying that he was living in Chicago, had been struggling for a while, which was why he'd never written before, but now he had landed on his feet, had a big apartment with a view of the lake, and wanted me to come and visit him. There'd be a train ticket in the letter, and ten dollars for dinner in the dining car and a cab to his apartment.

I never got any further than that in my imagination. I couldn't go any further, because he was the main part of the story and he was just a blank, a hole in the middle of the story. So I said to Sam, "I don't talk about him because there isn't anything to say."

"Doesn't your mom ever talk about him?"

"No. She doesn't want the subject brought up. She says, 'That's something best forgotten about, Gene. When you're older we can talk about it.'"

"It sounds to me like he was the one who did something bad, not your grampa."

"Why do you think that?" I said. "I don't think that. You don't know anything about him."

"Well, why won't your mom talk about him, then?"

I didn't want to hear anything bad about my dad, even though I didn't know him, wouldn't even recognize him if I saw him. "He didn't have to do anything bad. She just doesn't want to talk about him."

"All right," she said. "Maybe he didn't do anything bad. But I can see where he ties into this somehow. This oil guy, Gallen—it sounds like a swindle to me. Doesn't it to you, Gene? If there'd really ever been any oil at the Toffey place they'd have found it long ago, wouldn't they?"

She was chasing after the mystery again. I didn't much like the idea that my dad had been in on a swindle. "Maybe it wasn't a swindle. Maybe back then they had some reason to believe there was oil there."

Sam nodded. "That could be. But it still sounds like a swindle to me." She looked at her watch. "I've got to go. It's almost suppertime."

We could see that we were beginning to get somewhere in unraveling the mystery. We hadn't really found anything, but we were at least going in the right direction. Something had happened back then, something having to do with oil, the old Toffey place, and my dad. It was going to lead to Grampa.

We agreed that we'd start in on the papers again the next afternoon, and left. I walked with Sam as far as her house, and then I headed home along East Main Street. The sun was going down behind the tall elms along the road, so that pieces of light tumbled down through the branches and fell onto the road. It was a nice afternoon, but I didn't much notice it, for I was still thinking about my dad.

Why had he gone away? I'd always wondered if it had been because of me—something I'd done. Or maybe nothing I'd done—he just didn't like having a kid around. I knew that some grown-ups didn't like kids. Old Mrs. Marbury, who lived on the corner, was always shouting at kids for cutting across her lawn, or horsing around on the sidewalk in front of her house, or even whistling as they walked by. She just didn't like kids. Maybe my dad didn't like kids, and went away because of me. I hoped that wasn't so; I hoped he remembered me and wished he could visit me and take me out to the Cardinals game sometime, but couldn't because of some good reason he had.

I was pushing that thought away when there came that familiar tightening in my chest and the feeling of a small animal moving around inside of me. But this time I wasn't sorry, because I had a couple of questions to ask it. So I waited.

"Hello, Gene," the hollow voice came. "I hope we're in a better mood than last time."

Even though I had some questions I wanted to ask, I didn't want the voice to get the idea that I was feeling friendly toward it. "I'm never in a good mood when you come."

"It hurts me when you say things like that, Eugene. I have feelings, too, you know."

"I wish you had nicer feelings toward Grampa and me."

"Ah, me," the specter sighed. "And here I've come just to tell you how well you've been doing."

"What do you mean by that?" I said.

"This research task you and your little girl-friend have embarked on? I came to tell you that you're on the right track. Just keep going as you are."

I thought for a moment. I didn't want to attract the voice's attention to my dad, in case it'd decide to go after him, too. But there didn't seem to be any way around it. "What's my dad got to do with all of this?"

"Ah. And ah again. That is an interesting question, isn't it?"

I waited, but it didn't say anything more. "That's not an answer; it's just another question. Is he why you got me into this?"

"Your dad. Well now. Not a perfect human being. None of us is, of course, but your dad's imperfections were more apparent than most."

"I don't believe you. You don't think anyone is any good."

"True," the hollow voice said. "They aren't. Who can you name who's any good?"

"My mom. Grampa. There's two."

"In time you'll have another view of your grampa, I'm afraid, Gene."

"That's your opinion." I was beginning to feel pretty sore. "I don't believe a word you say. Especially about my dad."

"Ah well. Just keep on as you're going, you and your little girlfriend."

"She isn't my girlfriend; she's just a friend. And whether you like it or not, she has a name. Her name is Sam."

"I'll keep it in mind. Just go on as you are, Gene."

"Maybe I won't!" I shouted. "I don't have to do everything you tell me."

"Just keep going." And then it was gone.

I started walking home again, feeling confused and upset the way I always was when I'd got finished talking with the voice. Could it really make me hurt Grampa? How could it? And yet it had kept me from writing that letter for Sonny. What if the voice got me to kill Grampa? Forcing me to ram a knife into him or slug him over the head with a lead pipe? I shuddered and closed my eyes. How could I live with myself after I'd done something like that?

I was still feeling confused and restless after supper. I tried reading a book for a while, but I couldn't concentrate. I needed to talk to somebody, so I decided to go over to Sonny's. "Don't stay late," Mom said. "It's a school night. Have you finished your homework?"

"We didn't have any." I figured I could get up early and do it in the morning.

By the time I got to Sonny's it had gotten dark. We sat on the porch on the old car seat and swatted mosquitoes while we talked. Sonny's mom and his little sisters were inside listening to

Amos 'n' Andy on the radio. Every once in a while we could hear them laugh.

"Sonny, did your dad ever say anything about the old Toffey place up there on Spring Hollow Road?"

"Spring Hollow Road?"

"Where I used to live. Grampa owned a nice big house up there. The one on the corner. That was before I knew you." Sonny was actually a little older than me. He used to be a grade ahead of me, which was why I didn't know him back then. He'd got left back into our grade, and was mighty lucky he hadn't been left back more than that.

"The Toffey place?"

"Mom used to take me there berry picking. The house was empty, half the windows busted, the porch roof falling in, door wide open. When I was little, that old house scared me. Vacant windows like the eyes of some huge cat getting ready to pounce on me. Scared the pants off of me."

"Why'd the Toffey place come up all of a sudden?"

I looked around to make sure that Sonny's

mom couldn't hear me. "I've been looking in the old *Chronicle*s to see if I could find out anything about Grampa and what happened back then. Alice Samuels is helping me. The old Toffey place keeps popping up."

"How popping up?"

"Some guy bought it back around the time I was two, maybe a little after. He claimed there was oil there."

"What's that got to do with anything?" Sonny said.

"My dad was in on it."

"Well, *Yew*gene, I don't know nothing about your dad. You never told me nothing about him."

"I don't know anything about him, Sonny. They won't tell me anything."

"Won't tell you nothing about him?"

"Nothing. I don't even know if he's alive or dead."

"Could be dead, like my dad." Then he paused. "You know, Gene, I been thinking since Dad walked off of that lumber platform. I don't get this death stuff. What's the use of it? I don't see the need of it. Whose idea was it, anyway?"

"God's idea, I guess."

"I reckon there's no arguing with God, but all the same, I wish he hadn't of thought of it. Seems like an awful waste of people."

"Some people say they wouldn't want to live forever. They say they'd get tired of living."

"Yeah, sure," Sonny said. "People say they'll be glad to be dead, only not right away. They keep pushing it back until it gets to be forever by itself. As for me, I could do without death."

He was sad about his dad being dead, that was clear enough. Missed him, even though he hadn't been much use. He'd remember the few times they went fishing together, things like that, and forget about all the times he came up short with the money. "At least you had a dad for a while. I never had one at all. Not so's I can remember."

"You have your grampa."

"Yeah, he counts for something. Does stuff for me that a lot of dads wouldn't, I reckon." I didn't want to talk about this anymore. "Let's get back to the old Toffey place. Your dad ever mention it?"

"Well, now that you bring it up, I remember he did. He talked about it more'n once. Never said much about it, just that it was a good place to keep away from. He didn't talk about it all the time, but if the subject happened to come up, he'd say, 'That old Toffey farm's a good place to keep away from.'" Sonny thought a minute. "I'll tell you what, *Yew*gene, let's you and me go on out there and have a look around."

"I'm not going anywhere near that place in the dead of night," I said. "I've got enough problems with spooks as it is."

"I didn't mean tonight, for pete's sake, *Yew*-gene. I ain't going nowheres near that place at night, neither. What about tomorrow after school?"

I wanted to do it, but it scared me. Something had gone on in that house. I knew, and Sonny didn't. "Okay," I said. "We'll go on out there. If we don't feel like going inside we don't have to." But I was pretty sure we would.

. . .

I spoke to Sam at lunchtime. "I can't look at newspapers this afternoon. I've got something I have to do with Sonny."

"What's so important?"

I didn't want to tell her. She couldn't resist a mystery and would want to get in on it. She and Sonny weren't on the same wavelength and were likely to get into a fight. "It's sort of scary," I said.

"I won't be any more scared than you will," she said. "Where is it?"

"The old Toffey place we've been reading about in the *Chronicle*. Sonny says his dad always said it was a good place to stay away from. We decided to see why."

"You can't go out there without me, Gene. I knew about it before Sonny."

"Not if his dad used to say it was a good place to stay away from."

"Even so, I'm going," Sam said.

"You and Sonny aren't on the same wavelength. You'll argue over everything."

"No, we won't. I don't mind Sonny. If only he wouldn't curse so much."

"I've heard you curse," I said.

"That was by mistake. I don't chew grass and spit the way Sonny does. His manners aren't so hot."

"Manners aren't everything," I said. "If you're

worried about his manners you shouldn't come with us."

"I'm coming," she said. "It's just that Sonny isn't as smart as he ought to be."

"What do you mean by that? People can't ought to be smarter than they are."

"Sure they can," Sam said. "Sonny could be a lot smarter if he wanted to."

"Sonny's smart in his own way," I said. "You have to know him better."

"He isn't smart enough to keep his shirt tucked in and not chew grass."

"What's wrong with chewing grass? I chew grass sometimes."

"All right," she said. "Spitting."

"You have to spit, especially when you're playing baseball. It's part of the game, like keeping up a chatter. If you can't think of a reason to spit, you can always spit into your glove to keep it moist."

"Why is your glove supposed to be moist?" she said.

"Why do you have to argue about everything?" I said. "If you're going to argue about everything, you shouldn't come with us."

"I wasn't arguing. It was just a discussion. I'm coming. You can't stop me."

"I wasn't trying to stop you. I only said that you and Sonny aren't on the same wavelength."

"Well," she said, "I suppose it isn't his fault, considering the way he was raised. If only he'd comb his hair and keep his shirt tucked in."

I didn't answer that. She was bound and determined to come with us, even if she wasn't on the same wavelength as Sonny.

When I told Sonny that Sam was coming with us he groaned. "She's more stuck-up than a pin cushion."

"Stop groaning about it, Sonny. She isn't as stuck-up as she pretends. She's a girl; she likes things neat and tidy."

"Too tidy for me," Sonny said. "I never saw the use of being neat and tidy. If everyone was neat and tidy there wouldn't be no tennis balls lying around the country club."

"You're just not on the same wavelength as her," I said.

"Well, I suppose she can't help it. It's the way she was raised."

So it was settled that Sam would come with

us, as much as anything ever got settled. After school the three of us walked out to Spring Hollow Road. It had clouded over and some wind had come up. It felt like rain. Sonny and Sam were being as polite as could be in order to show that they could be on the same wavelength with each other and prove me wrong. Sam would say, "What did your dad say was wrong with the Toffey place, Sonny? I don't believe in haunts or anything like that. There isn't any good evidence for them." And instead of Sonny saying something sarcastic the way he usually did, like, "You'd believe in 'em fast enough if one was after you," he would say, "Well, I don't know, Sam, you might be right about that." It was unnatural to them both, and I wished they'd quit it, but it was my own fault for telling them they weren't on the same wavelength with each other. I could see where soon enough they'd be ganging up on me. But I let it go.

Spring Hollow Road was a good two miles out of town, and it took us a while to walk there, going past a couple of farms and stretches of woods. The sky was getting darker, and we began to wonder if we ought to turn back; but we were almost there and didn't want to give up now. Finally we came to the corner where Spring Hollow Road turned off from the blacktop road. Grampa's grand old house was on the corner. I hadn't seen it for a while. It didn't look much different. They'd blacktopped the driveway that circled up to the big columns at the doorway, the door was painted green instead of brown-stained, and there was a new Pontiac parked out front, but that was about it. I wondered who lived there now. Was some little kid up there in my room playing with a train set or building a castle with blocks the way I'd done? I didn't know if I liked that idea, and I pushed it out of my mind. "Remember when I lived here, Sam? Remember jumping rope on that lawn?"

"Sort of," she said. "We were pretty little."

"Hey," Sonny said. "I thought we came up here to explore the Toffey house, not stand around remembering old times."

We started down Spring Hollow Road. Still a dirt road—no point in paving it. Now I felt some nervousness come on, a light prickling in my stomach. The vacant old house had always scared me, but now that I knew it had some connection to the voice, my dad, Grampa, and Mr. Hawkins walking off into midair, it scared me more than ever. My heart was thumping and my face was sweaty.

We went on walking, and after a little while we began to come in sight of the old house—dark, vacant eyes—and behind it, sticking up over the roof, a couple of tall spruce trees, green against the gray-black sky. We trudged on a little more, until we were standing in front of it—lawn all grown up with brush, roof sagging down in the middle, chimneys tipped, porch roof fallen down at one end, the roof posts for that part lying across the porch floor.

"Well, there it is," Sonny said. "I don't think I was ever out here before."

"Me neither," Sam said.

"Didn't you ever come berry picking with my mom and me, Sam?"

She shook her head. "Not that I recall. Did you ever go inside, Gene?"

"No. I was always too scared."

For a moment the three of us stood there staring at the old house. We all knew that we had to go in, but none of us was in any hurry to do it.

"I've been in places like this before," Sonny said. "There was an old shack by the river where some hermit died. Nobody wanted to go in there, but me and Dad went in to see if there was anything worth hooking. Found a nice piece of one-inch rope, a saw, and an ax. There was some clothes there, too, pants and shirts, but Dad wouldn't touch 'em. Said he wasn't gonna wear no dead man's clothes."

"We don't know if anyone died in the Toffey place," Sam said.

But I did. Or was pretty sure of it, anyway. "Well, if we're going in, we better do it before it starts raining." And in fact, we could hear the rumbling of thunder in the distance.

We walked through the brush growing in the lawn, and up onto the porch. From here we could stare through the empty windows into the living room. Not much to see—broken glass on the floor, a fireplace with cold ashes still in it, a flight of stairs going up, curtains on one of the windows blowing around a little in the breeze. "Not much to see here," Sonny said.

"A lot of times these mysterious old places aren't so mysterious when you look at them objectively," Sam said.

Sonny gave her a look. "My dad said it was a good place to stay away from. I expect there's something to what he said."

"I'm not saying there isn't, Sonny," Sam said. "But you have to be objective about it."

This was a little more natural: being polite all the time was too much of a strain for them both. "Let's go in and find out," I said. I stepped through the door. What with the rain clouds above, it was fairly dark in that living room, but there was enough light to see by. "Nothing here," I said.

Through a door at the back of the living room we could see the corner of an old iron stove. "Kitchen," I said. We went back there. Nothing much there, either—more broken glass, the old stove, old kitchen cabinets with glass windows in them, a coffee mug in the gray stone sink, dust everywhere, a wooden chair with a leg broken off that hadn't been worth moving when the widow Toffey left. On the floor there was a scrap of newspaper. I scooped it up.

"What is it?" Sam said.

I glanced over it. "It's about this guy Gallen who was saying that there was oil out here. He was wanted for questioning. It says, 'Questions have been raised by investors in Gallen's oil syndicate. The office of the attorney general is investigating and wishes to question Gallen.' That's the whole article."

"Is there a date on it?" Sam asked.

"Yeah. October 10, 1925," I said.

"Let me see that clipping, Gene."

"Don't you believe me?"

"I believe you. I just want to see the typeface." I handed her the clipping. "It's not from the *Chronicle*. That's not our typeface. A St. Louis paper, maybe. Or Chicago. Maybe even Kansas City."

"We looked through the *Chronicle* for that year," I said. "It's funny your dad didn't run a story on it."

"There's probably an explanation," Sam said. "Otherwise my dad would have run something." She looked around. "I guess kids must have been out here breaking windows," she said.

"It wasn't no kids," Sonny said. "Otherwise there'd be stones around the floor."

There came another rumble of thunder. "We'd better finish exploring and get out of here before it starts to rain," I said. I took the clipping from Sam, folded it, and put it into my back pocket. We trooped out of the kitchen back into the living room, and started up the stairs. At the top there was a little hall with two doors opening off it. Sonny gave one of the doors a kick, and it swung open. We peered in. Nothing except more broken glass. That was all. "Not much mystery so far," Sam said.

There came a loud crack of thunder. "Let's get out of here," Sonny said.

"There's one more room," Sam said.

"Okay, then we go," Sonny said. "I don't aim on getting soaked."

We turned, and Sonny kicked this door open. For a moment we stood and stared.

"Holy Christmas," Sonny whispered.

Dangling from the light fixture in the ceiling was a rope tied in a hangman's noose. On the floor underneath it were a man's clothes, neatly in place, as if a headless man had lain down there—pink striped shirt, brown pants, black socks still in his shoes—rotted here and there, but otherwise neat and tidy. And inside the clothes were his bones—ribs holding the shirt up, finger bones at the end of the shirtsleeves, leg bones visible between the cuffs of his pants and the top of his socks.

About a yard away lay his skull, tipped sideways, so that the eye sockets stared directly at us. The jawbone had fallen off and was lying beside the skull.

Then came a flash of lightning and a huge crack of thunder. We let out a howl and then we were tumbling down the stairs, racing through the living room, across the porch, through the brush in the yard, and on down Spring Hollow Road. We didn't stop running until we were back in front of Grampa's old house at the corner of the blacktop road.

Chapter 7

We stood at the corner in front of Grampa's old house, gasping for breath and looking at one another. A whole lot of questions were whirling around in my mind, going so fast I couldn't catch hold of any of them. "Sonny," I said finally, "do you think your dad knew about— knew what was in that room?"

"I don't know. He never said nothing about it. I'd have remembered that and would have gone to have a look a long time ago."

"But some people in Magnolia must have known about it," I said. "How could you keep it a secret?"

"Not necessarily," Sam said. "He might have gone up there all alone and committed suicide."

Sonny shook his head. "Didn't commit suicide. You got to have a chair or a table to jump off of to hang yourself. Wasn't anything in that room you could jump from."

"Maybe there was some furniture there at the time," Sam said. "Maybe people came along later and hooked it."

"They wouldn't have," I said. "Whoever did would have told everybody in town that there was a corpse out there hanging from the ceiling. The state troopers would have taken him away." A spit of rain hit my cheek. "We better get going," I said.

We started walking back toward town at a good pace. "That's just the point," Sam said. "If somebody had got lynched in Magnolia, it'd be hard to keep it quiet."

"Especially if the lynching had to do with this oil guy," I said.

Suddenly Sonny stared at us. "Oil," he said. "What was that all about, exactly?"

"As far as Gene and I can figure it out," Sam said, "this guy Ernest Gallen came down from Chicago and bought the Toffey place from old widow Toffey. Then he began telling everybody there was oil under the land there, and got them to put their money into it."

"Invest in it," I said. "I guess they would have needed money for oil wells and stuff."

"I know something else," Sonny said. "My dad was in on it, too."

We all stopped walking. "Your dad?"

"Yeah," he said. "My dad. He had this big old yellow envelope he kept tucked away in his dresser drawer. He used to take it out every once in a while and stare at it. Just stare at it. And then put it away in his dresser drawer again. Once Mom told me that they was oil certificates. Dad had sold everything he could lay his hands on to raise the money for them—his watch, his little old fishing boat, an old Model T he had back then. Couldn't get much for the stuff, Mom said, but nobody'd lend him any money to buy them oil certificates with. Mom said they was worthless and to forget about them." He looked at me. "You think your specter has something to do with them oil certificates?"

He'd forgot that Sam didn't know about the specter. I gave her a quick glance. "I don't know," I said.

But nothing got past Sam. "What specter?" she said.

"Blame me, Gene," Sonny said. "I figured you'd told her."

Sam looked from me to Sonny. "What specter?" She looked at me again. "What's this all about?"

To be honest, I was just as glad to tell her. In a funny way, the more people who knew about the voice, the more protected I felt from it. I couldn't tell Mom and Grampa; they'd never believe me and they'd probably ship me off to a nut doctor. But Sam would believe me. "I've got a voice inside me, Sam."

She squinted her whole face and stared at me through the squint. "What? A voice?"

"It isn't there all the time. It comes every two or three days to talk to me."

"Who comes?"

"The voice. The specter. It's the spirit of somebody. I think maybe it's the spirit of that guy who was hung up there in the Toffey house. Or maybe it's someone else. The voice won't tell me. It says I have to find out for myself so I'd be convinced."

She went on staring at me through her squint. "What do you mean, a voice? Where's it coming from?"

"It's inside of me. Inside my head."

"I don't see how that can be," she said. "Are you sure you aren't just hearing things?"

"Oh, it's real, all right. It can make me do things I don't want to do."

"How?"

"I don't know how. It just can."

She stopped squinting and wrinkled her forehead. "Why did this voice pick on you, especially?"

"Because of my grampa. I think it wants me to kill him."

"Kill your grampa? You wouldn't do that, Gene."

"I don't know," I said. "It's pretty strong when it gets its claws into you. It killed Sonny's dad."

"What?"

Sonny nodded. "The voice told him to walk off that lumber platform. He knew it was trying to kill him, because it told him to dive in front of a car once. He said it had a grip on him so strong he couldn't resist. He was all set to dive, but the driver saw him leaning out into the road and hit the brakes in time. Dad said that afterwards he was as weak as a kitten and covered with sweat."

Nobody said anything for a minute. It was spitting a bit of rain and we started to walk again, this time more quickly. "Isn't there anything you can do to make it go away, Gene?"

"Sure doesn't seem like it."

There was more silence. Then Sam asked, "Aren't you scared, Gene?"

"I sure am. I walk around scared out of my pants half the time. Scared when the voice is talking to me, and when it isn't there, I'm scared it will come. I'm blame tired of being scared day in and day out."

"Dad said he was scared, too. Scared to death. Said he knew the voice was gonna get him in the end, though. Said he was fighting it as hard as he could, but he didn't think it would be any use."

"It hasn't come after you, Sonny?" Sam said.

"No. I guess it was satisfied with killing Dad and is willing to leave the rest of us be. Wouldn't be any point in going after my little sisters anyway. They ain't worth killing, even the two added together."

"You shouldn't say things like that, Sonny," Sam said.

"I reckon there's a lot of things I shouldn't ought to say."

There was more silence. Then Sam said, "Sonny, we've got to help Gene. We've got to help him get out of this."

"I reckon we should," Sonny said. "I just wish I could see a way how."

"Maybe you shouldn't help me. Maybe the voice will come after you if you help me."

"Sonny and I'll have to chance it," Sam said. "That's all there is to it."

"What I don't get," Sonny said, "is that the body must have been rotting out there for months. A thing like that makes an awful stink. You ever smell a dead possum by the roadside? How come nobody smelled it and reported it to the police?"

"Hardly anybody goes down there," I said. "No reason to."

"But somebody must have gone down there once in a while," Sonny said. "Maybe somebody who knew about the berry bushes, same as you did, Gene."

"They were covering it up, Sonny," Sam said. "That's the way I see it. Gene and I have been through a whole bunch of old *Chronicle*s and we didn't see anything at all about a lynching, or the oil swindler getting arrested."

"It figures, don't it, Sam?" Sonny said. "They wouldn't bring that body in, for once you got a body you got to do something about it. Blame hard to pretend nothing happened when you got a corpse laying in the back of your pickup truck. So they decided to leave it out there to rot."

Sam shuddered. "What a terrible thing to do."

Sonny nodded. "Seems so to me, too," he said. "Hard enough on a fellow to get lynched. Worse when you was left to rot instead of being buried proper."

Sam nodded vigorously. "If you're going to lynch a guy, at least you ought to have the goodness to bury him. Everybody deserves that much."

"Well," I said, "maybe we shouldn't be too

quick to blame people. We don't know what happened yet."

"I'm going to see what I can get out of Dad," Sam said. "He knows a lot of things he never puts in the paper. He's bound to know about this oil well guy."

"He won't tell you, Sam," I said. "They've been covering this thing up from the beginning."

"I'll worm it out of him," she said. "I'm good at worming things out of him."

By now the rain was spitting pretty hard. We began to trot, and left off talking in order to save our breath for getting home. Soon I was in our house, feeling kind of damp. Nobody was at home. I went upstairs to the bathroom to dry myself off. I had hardly started rubbing my head with a towel when I felt that pressure come, and the little movements inside of me. "I knew you'd be coming," I said. "After what we saw today."

"You're right about that, Eugene. What did you think of it?"

"That was you who they hung, wasn't it? You didn't commit suicide. Somebody lynched you." From down below I heard a car pull up in front of the house. It sounded like Grampa's Model A.

"You're a smart boy, Gene. I like the way you think."

A car door slammed. "If I let out to everybody that you were lynched, will you get off my back?"

"There are a few other small things I'll need you to do, as well."

I heard somebody come into the house. "It's Grampa." There were footsteps on the stairs.

"Yes, Grampa. He's high on the list. We've got to do something about him."

"I'm not going to kill Grampa, if that's what you're thinking." But the tightening was already loosening, and the specter was sliding away. The bathroom door opened. Hastily I began drying my hair again, and turned my head to look. Mom was standing there. "I went to the park with Sonny and Sam," I said. "We got caught in the rain on the way home."

Mom was frowning at me. "Gene, did I hear you say something about Grampa?"

Of course what I'd said was that I *wasn't*

going to kill Grampa, but either way it would have sounded pretty bad to her. "What do you think I said?"

"Something about killing Grampa. I heard it plain as day. You were talking quite loudly."

"Mom, I never said anything like that. You must have misheard."

"I certainly hope so. You've been talking to yourself a lot lately. Talking in a loud voice as if somebody were there with you."

I would have to learn to lower my voice when I was talking to the specter. "People talk to themselves, Mom. I've heard you talk to yourself in the store. 'Oh, look at what they're charging for tomatoes now,' and 'I guess I better take four cans of beans as long as they're on sale.' I've heard you say stuff like that."

"Yes, I admit it. I talk to myself like that sometimes. But not the way you did, in a loud voice as if somebody were actually there. This is something new."

I had to get out of this conversation. "Mom, I've always talked to myself. I didn't realize I was being so loud about it."

She didn't say anything for a minute. Then

she said, "Well, all right. Put on a dry shirt. We'll be having supper shortly."

But I knew that wouldn't be the end of it because she was bound to discuss it with Grampa, and he'd want to have a talk with me.

The next afternoon I went over to the *Chronicle* office with Sonny and Sam. I'd never expected them to become friends.

Sam was bound and determined to go to college and become a brilliant mathematician or a brilliant archaeologist—it didn't seem to matter much what it was, so long as it had "brilliant" in front of it. Sonny was hardly likely to finish high school—always said he would, but I knew Sonny. Along about the time he got to be fifteen he'd start skipping school a lot: every time there was a nice morning he'd decide it'd be more interesting to laze under the willow tree with his dad's fishing pole than sit in a stuffy classroom learning to do square roots. By and by he'd have missed so many days there'd be no chance he'd pass. The idea of repeating a grade he'd hardly been to in the first place would be too much for him, and that'd be the end of school for Sonny.

But I could see that they were curious about

each other. Sam had never known anyone like Sonny. Sonny wasn't the kind of kid who got asked to nice birthday parties where they had hot dogs, paper hats, ice cream, and a cake with the right number of candles on it. Sonny barely went to his own birthday, much less anyone else's. His dad would give him a couple of fishing lures he was likely to use himself, his mom would make him his favorite—spaghetti and meatballs—and that would be about it.

But Sam could see there was value to Sonny, even though he chewed grass, spit, and let his shirttail hang out. She said to me once, "Sonny's a whole lot smarter than you would figure. I'm getting used to his shirttail and chewing grass. I just wish he wouldn't spit so much."

On the other side of it, Sonny was mighty curious about Sam. In a way, she was as foreign to him as a French or Siamese person would be. I spoke good English, or was supposed to, anyway, and tucked my shirttail in, but Sonny knew that I didn't have much more money than he did—didn't get an allowance the way Sam did, and had to pay for baseballs and gloves myself, same as him. I was more on his side of the fence.

Of course we played baseball with kids from nice homes like Sam's—but everybody was glad enough to have Sonny on their team, even if his shirttail was out and his English wasn't so hot. But he didn't hang around with those kids much—wasn't asked to their birthday parties or to go to the movies with them, which they could afford because they had allowances.

Now he was hanging around with Sam, and he was curious about her. What was it like to have two or three pairs of shoes, a couple of extra shirts, a nice warm coat with all the buttons on it for winter? What was it like to have a dad who people in town looked up to? What was it like to be on the inside of town, rather than hanging around on the edges picking up leftovers—secondhand clothes, an old bike you had to fix up yourself with wires and tape?

But he'd got to know her better, and I guess when you know people you're more likely to get friendly with them, even if they're different from you. Of course, they argued a lot—wouldn't have seemed natural if they hadn't. But that was okay: it spared me having to argue with Sam—let Sonny do it.

At least this time we had some idea of what we were looking for. We took down the papers from around the time of the hanging—October 1925—and started going through them, just to make sure we hadn't missed something. But we hadn't. There wasn't anything in the paper about the lynching—not for the week that it happened, nor the one for the week after, nor the week after that.

"Maybe we got something wrong," Sonny said when we'd given up looking.

"Like what?" I said.

"Like maybe that guy who got lynched didn't have nothing to do with the story in the newspaper we found out there. That piece of newspaper could of got dropped some other time, not when they was lynching him."

"Maybe," Sam said. "There's another explanation, though."

"What's that?" I asked.

"What if my dad knew all about the lynching and decided not to put it in the paper."

"Would he do that? Leave an important story like that out of the paper?"

"Sure. He does it all the time. Like when the

deacon got caught robbing the church's bank account to pay for his gambling, Dad didn't put it in. The family was still living in Magnolia. Dad said they didn't need the shame of it."

"So you think he might have left the lynching out on purpose? Wouldn't people have thought it was funny that the story wasn't in the paper?"

"Maybe nobody knew," Sonny said. "Maybe the only ones who knew were the ones who did it."

We were quiet for a minute. "Sam," I said, "what about asking your dad about it?"

"If they was covering it up, he won't tell you nothing," Sonny said.

"That's probably right," Sam said. "If he wouldn't put it in the paper, he isn't going to tell me. He knows I can't keep my mouth shut."

"Try anyway, Sam." I said. "It was a long time ago. Maybe nobody cares about it now. You said you were good at worming things out of him."

She shrugged. "I can try."

So we left it at that, and a couple of days later she told us about it. "I asked him if there was some kind of hanging here in about 1925.

He said, 'I thought you kids were working on a school project. What kind of school project is it?' And I told him that the hanging wasn't a school project; we just heard about it. He said, 'Where'd you hear about it?' I told him Sonny Hawkins got it from his dad. And Dad said, 'Since when are you such a big pal of Sonny Hawkins?'"

Sonny gave her a look. "You don't have to be a pal of mine if you don't want to. I don't need anyone for a pal."

"I didn't say that, Sonny," Sam said. "I told Dad you were okay even if you didn't comb your hair and your shirttail was always out. I said we weren't supposed to judge people on their appearances anyway, only on the inside of their souls. He said I was right, probably Daniel Boone didn't comb his hair or tuck his shirttail in."

Sonny reached behind himself and started tucking his shirttail in. Then he thought better of it and pulled his shirttail out again.

"Let's get off Sonny's shirttail," I said. "What else did your dad say?"

"Nothing. Every time I tried to get him onto

the hanging he swung around to something else. I couldn't get him to admit anything."

"I thought you were so hot at worming him."

"Yeah, so did I. But I couldn't worm him on this."

"But you figure he knew about it?"

"I think so," she said.

Well, we didn't know where we were with it, except that I was in a heap of trouble. It made me feel more comfortable with myself to have Sam and Sonny on my side, but really, what could they do for me? They couldn't do anything about the specter. And we couldn't find out much about anything else if the grown-ups were going to cover up the whole thing. When I had Sonny and Sam around, it didn't seem so bad—seemed almost hopeful. Sam was the hopeful type anyway, always sure there was a way out of anything. But when I was alone, it didn't seem so hopeful. It was like I'd been abandoned by everybody.

A day later, Grampa pinned me down for a chat. I was coming in from delivering groceries for Snuffy. As usual, Grampa was reading the *Post-Dispatch*. He folded it in his lap. "Gene, sit down for a minute. I want to have a chat."

There was a footstool by his chair that I could have sat in, but I felt like standing up. Grampa took off his reading glasses and looked at me. "Gene, your mom says you've been talking to yourself a lot recently."

"I don't think it's a lot," I said. "Just the normal amount. Everybody talks to themselves sometimes. Mom even does."

"Yes, that's certainly true. But your mom says this isn't the usual thing. She says it seems as if you're arguing with somebody who isn't there. Some kind of imaginary person. She said it's as if you're trying to convince yourself of something. Talk yourself into something."

I tried to think of some excuse. "I guess maybe it's because of what happened to Sonny's dad. That's kind of hard to get over."

Grampa nodded. "That's understandable. It was a very unhappy business. It's natural that it would bother you. Your mom and I have considered that. But your mom said she's heard you arguing with yourself before."

"Grampa, I don't remember talking to myself all that much." I wished Mom would say supper was ready, but I knew she was holding off until Grampa had finished talking to me.

"Your mom remembers it pretty clearly, because it worried her. She didn't understand it. Now she says she overheard you saying something about killing me."

"Grampa, I wouldn't do anything like that."

"Gene, I don't believe for a minute that you want to kill me, or anyone else, for that matter. I'm curious to know why you said it."

"I didn't say it, Grampa. Mom misheard." That, at least was true; I'd said just the opposite, that I wouldn't kill Grampa.

"She doesn't think she misheard." He was silent for a moment. Then he said, "Gene, who did you think you were arguing with?"

"I didn't think I was arguing with anybody."

"That isn't what your mom says."

I felt ashamed of myself for all these lies, and sick of the whole thing. Why couldn't they leave me alone? "If you won't believe me, what can I say?"

"Gene, I'm not calling you a liar. We think something's bothering you, and we'd like to help you. I don't care what you did, or think you did. We love you and we always will. But we want you to tell us what's troubling you so we can help you deal with it."

"There's nothing to tell, Grampa. Nothing's bothering me."

He didn't say anything for a bit. Then he said, "All right, Gene. I'll take your word for it. But remember, anytime you want to talk about something, we're here to listen." He got up. "I'll go see how your mom is doing with supper."

. . .

When I got to school on Monday, I went looking for Sam to see if she'd been able to worm anything more out of her dad. But she wasn't in school. I had to wait until second period, when we went to science, to ask somebody. "Where's Samuels?" I said.

"Didn't you hear? Her dad got into an awful car crash. He drove off the road into a tree. Nobody can figure out how it happened. It was in the middle of the afternoon, a nice clear day, and not much traffic."

I went cold. "Is he dead?"

"No. They say he'll be okay. But he was hurt pretty bad."

"And they don't know what happened? He didn't blow out a tire or anything?"

"No. Mr. Samuels doesn't drink, either. Some trucker coming along behind him said that he was sailing along perfectly well. Suddenly he veered off the road into a tree. Luckily, the trucker got him out of the wreck and took him to the hospital. Nobody can figure it out."

But I could.

Chapter 8

It took me two days to get hold of Sam. I called her two or three times, and then I finally walked over to her house to see if she was there. She said she was spending a lot of time in the hospital with her dad, and the rest of the time she was helping her mom by doing the laundry and cleaning up around the house. She said she was going to stay home from school for a couple more days to help, but that she could meet us down at the bandstand for a little while around four o'clock the next afternoon.

Sonny and I got there right on time. Hot day, but it was cooler on the bandstand in the shade of the big elms. Sam came running up five minutes later. "Sorry," she said. "I had to finish hanging up the clothes. I didn't know that being a mom was so much work. I'm going to be a brilliant heart surgeon instead."

"How's your dad?" Sonny said. "He going to be okay?"

"I guess so," she said. "He broke one of his legs in two places. The doctor said he might have a limp. Everybody says he's lucky to get off that lightly after an accident like that."

Sonny and I both wanted to know the same thing, but we weren't sure if we should ask. "Was it a blowout?" I said. "A sudden blowout can make your car veer."

"No. It wasn't a blowout. You know what it was." She looked scared.

"You sure?" Sonny said.

"Dad was unconscious when he got to the hospital, and they took him into the operating room right away and put him under ether. He didn't talk much the first couple of days. Mostly he dozed. Ate a little soup and dozed some more. But then he felt like talking a little. He made arrangements with Mom about who was to run the newspaper while he was laid up. And he started to talk about it. For one thing, he was afraid people might decide he had been drunk. He hardly drinks at all. Has a bottle of beer sometimes on a real hot day. He said it wouldn't be good for the newspaper if people decided it was run by a drunk. So he hadn't had anything to drink; he just couldn't explain what happened. He was going along on the road out to East Creek. There was an old Civil War veteran having his ninetieth birthday and Dad wanted to do a story on him for the *Chronicle*. Just an everyday story, the kind he'd been writing for years. Nothing special. He was going along, maybe thirty-five miles an hour, when all of a sudden he felt this tightness in his chest, a sort of pressure. For a moment he thought it might be a heart attack, but it didn't feel like any heart attack he'd ever heard of. A heart attack is pretty painful, he said, and this wasn't painful, just a pressure."

"Yes, that's it," I said. "Just a tightness but no pain."

She nodded. "About that time he noticed a big tree along the side of the road about a quarter of a mile away. And suddenly he started thinking, 'What if I ran off the road into that tree?' He didn't know why he was thinking that. He told himself to cut it out, but every time he tried to think of something else, the same thought kept coming back—'What if I ran into that tree?' The tightness kept growing and the tree began racing toward him, and the next thing he knew he was waking up in his hospital bed feeling sick from the ether."

None of us said anything, but we looked at one another. "Did you tell him about the specter?"

"No. I knew he wouldn't believe me." She looked at Sonny and me, scared and white. "What are we going to do? Is the voice going to kill everybody?"

"No," Sonny said. "It ain't gonna kill everybody. Just the ones that were in on the lynching."

"My dad wouldn't have lynched anybody."

"No, but he helped to cover it up," Sonny said.

"What about your dad, Sonny?" Sam asked.

"I don't know. I hope he wasn't in on it. It seems to me like he was too lazy to get in on a lynching. But he owned them oil certificates.

Maybe he got took for a ride along with the rest."

"What about my grampa?" I said. "He was a judge back then. He wouldn't have lynched anyone."

"Maybe he sentenced this oil guy who got lynched to jail."

It was possible, but we didn't know. We sat there on the seats on the bandstand, thinking. Finally Sonny said, "Know what I think? I think we oughta go back out there to that old house and have another look around. We scampered outta there pretty quick. We might of missed something."

"You really want to go out there again, Sonny?" Sam said.

"Well, you know, Sam, this is about the most interesting thing that ever happened to me. I'd kinda like to see how it ends up. Ain't nothing much ever happens around Magnolia, and ain't nothing likely to. I ain't ready to quit on this yet."

"I am," I said. "I'd quit tomorrow if the specter'd let me."

"Well, yeah, Gene," Sonny said. "You got a

particular interest in it. I can see where you might want to chuck the whole thing. But seeing as you can't, we might as well keep going. It seems to me we oughta get a better look at that old Toffey house."

I shrugged. "If Sonny's willing, I guess I am."

Sam nodded. "I guess Sonny's right. We'd better go back out there. I don't like the idea too much, but I can see that we ought to."

We had to wait until Saturday. Sam's dad came home from the hospital that morning, so Sam's mom could stay home and Sam was freed up a little. This time we brought flashlights with us. At least Sam and I did: Sonny didn't have a flashlight — not one that worked, anyway. It was the middle of the afternoon and the sun was bright. We'd planned it that way because we had no intention of being caught out there after the sun went down.

We walked out to the house. For a moment we stood at the edge of the brushy lawn looking at that old place. It stared back at us out of its empty eyes — old gray boards, crooked chimney, sagging roof, like an evil creature with a hunched back, big crooked teeth, rotten breath.

We weren't in much of a rush to cross the lawn and go inside again. But then Sonny said, "Well? What are we waiting for?" So we went through the brush and tall grass on the lawn, across the porch, and into the living room. Here we flashed our lights around. Nothing new. We went into the kitchen and did the same. Nothing we hadn't seen before.

The kitchen door was hanging open. We went out into the backyard—what used to be a backyard, anyway. The three big spruce trees loomed high overhead, turning the yard into a kind of dark cave. A rusty fifty-gallon oil drum sat on a wooden rack by the back door. Probably held kerosene for the stoves once. Sonny banged on the drum to see if it was empty. At the hollow sound a little milk snake slithered out from under the drum and disappeared into the tall grass. "I don't like snakes," Sam said. "Let's go in."

Sonny grinned. "Probably a bunch of snakes inside, too." Sam gave him a dirty look, but she didn't say anything. We went back in. We all knew we were stalling: none of us wanted to visit those headless bones again. Finally Sam said, "We may as well do it, fellas. Let's go upstairs."

We went up the stairs and crowded into the doorway of that room. It was as still as death in there, the noose hanging down from the light fixture, unmoving; the clothes empty of everything but bones. Nothing moved. Nothing had moved there for years. Everything had lain dead still as the sun came up and shone in and went down; as the moon rose, its pale light passing over the skull and going down; as winter came, the snow had fallen and melted; and then spring came, wildflowers bloomed again, as the years rolled by. Had the specter been wandering around all that time looking for a way to get even? Did it know we were there now, staring at its bones? Was it watching us? I felt a chill go over my back. "Let's get going so we can get out of here," I said.

Sonny walked around the clothes to the noose and took a look at it. "It ain't a proper hangman's noose. You can't slide a hangman's noose open—got to cut it."

"How do you know that, Sonny?" Sam said.

"My dad used to buy them cowboy magazines sometimes. I read enough cowboy stories to know how a noose works. Somebody could've opened up this noose and let him drop."

Sam and I pushed into the room to examine the noose. "Who would have done it?"

"I don't reckon nobody did it," Sonny said. "If somebody had dropped him here the skull would have still been attached to the neck. Looks to me more like he rotted for a while and then the body pulled loose from the head and fell. Head dropped and rolled away a little."

Sam and I both shuddered. Then the three of us stooped over the clothes. "Look," Sonny said, pointing. "Neck's all tore up." It was true: the neck bones were not lying in a neat line, but were lying in a jumble.

Now Sam reached out gingerly and touched the collar of the pink shirt. I don't know what we thought might happen, but nothing did. She closed her hand around the collar and gave it a little tug. The shirt had rotted in places, and tore over the ribs. The arm bone slid a few inches out of the sleeve, disturbing the finger bones. Sam pulled the shirt away. More rotten cloth tore and bones clattered onto the floor. She stood, holding the half-rotted shirt. On the floor beneath lay the rib cage, scattered back bones, arm bones, finger bones.

There was a splotch of blood on the front of the shirt, near the collar. "He must of been fighting them off," Sonny said. "Got a busted nose or something."

The shirt had a breast pocket. "See if there's anything in the pocket, Sam," I said.

"You look, Gene. I pulled the shirt out of there."

I took the shirt, put my fingers into the pocket, and pulled out a piece of paper folded in half. I unfolded it and saw some pencil scribbling:

```
Ernie—
I will talk to the judge as soon as I
can about your bail. Keep up your
spirits.
                              —Tom
```

Tom. "My dad's name."

"So this oil guy, Gallen, was in jail," Sonny said.

"Let's not talk about it now," Sam said. "Let's

get finished with these clothes and get out of here. I'm getting the creeps."

I looked at the others. "My turn, I guess." I stooped over the clothes, took hold of the pants by one of the belt loops, and pulled them away. Again, some rotten cloth tore. The leg bones dropped down out of the pants, and the pelvis tipped out, bounced on the floor, and rolled away a little distance.

"Anything in them pants?" Sonny asked.

I held the pants out to him. "You do it. I did the shirt pocket."

He took the pants, pushed his hand into a side pocket, and pulled out a handkerchief splotched with dark red blood. "They must've banged him around some," he said. He put the handkerchief back in the pocket, reached into the other side pocket, and came out with some coins. "Two quarters and a nickel," he said.

"Fifty-five cents. You going to keep it, Sonny?"

"Not me," he said. "I ain't stealing money from no dead man. Someone else can have it." He slid the coins back into the pocket and reached into the back pocket. This time he drew out a newspaper clipping. He unfolded it, gave it a quick look, and handed it to me.

Questions Raised About Magnolia Oil Claim

Reports that oil has been discovered in the town of Magnolia, thirty miles west of St. Louis, have been questioned by federal authorities, according to a spokesman for the Department of the Interior, Mr. Elliot Smith. Studies by geologists for the Department of the Interior conclude that there is little likelihood of significant oil deposits in the Magnolia area or surrounding territory. Mr. Ernest Gallen, who insists that he possesses valid geological reports showing oil deposits beneath land he owns in Magnolia, says, "This is a typical example of government interference with the rights of American citizens. I have complete faith in the reports made by my geologists, as we shall soon discover

when drilling operations start next
month."

However, investors in the project
have become alarmed, and many are
demanding their money back. According
to Mr. Thomas Richards, a spokesman
for the Gallen operation, "We will
happily return the money of anyone
who wants it. We have plenty of other
people who will be glad to take
advantage of this great opportunity."
Asked when investors might be receiving
their money, Richards said it would
be done "in a few days, when we finish
the necessary paperwork."

Sam and Sonny looked at me. "That was
your dad, Gene?"

"I guess so," I said. I'd never even known my
dad, hadn't much idea of him, but still I didn't
like the idea that he'd been in on a swindle. He
was still my dad—might write me a letter someday, with a railroad ticket in it so I could come
to visit him in his fancy apartment in Chicago.
"He might not have known there was anything

crooked about it. He might have thought it was on the up-and-up."

Sam and Sonny looked at me. I could tell they didn't believe it. "Most likely that was it, Gene," Sam said. "Your dad didn't know it was crooked."

I decided to change the subject. "Sam, what newspaper is this from?" I handed her the clipping. She looked it over. "I don't know," she said. "It wasn't the *Chronicle*." She frowned. "I wish I could understand why my dad covered all this up. Kept it out of the newspaper."

"He probably had a good reason, Sam," I said.

We were quiet, and then Sonny said, "I reckon they all thought they had good reasons for what they was doing. Half the town might of been in on it as far as we know. Every one of 'em with a good reason. Never any shortage of good reasons when you need one."

"What about your dad, Sonny?" Sam said. "What was his good reason for being in on it?"

"Wanted some free money. There ain't nothin' people like better than free money. They'll do most anything for money they don't have to work for. Most people think they got a right to free money if they think there's any around. I don't guess my dad was any different from the rest."

"That doesn't explain why the voice wanted to kill him."

Sonny didn't say anything for a while, but looked down at the bones all tumbled around on the floor. "I guess it embarrassed him a good deal to have got swindled out of his free money. Reckon he might not have been sorry to see this here Gallen get it stuck to him."

That was as close as he was going to come to admitting that his dad had been in on the lynching. I figured that was a subject we might as well stay off of, too. "What are we going to do with these clothes? Just leave them here?"

"I sure don't want 'em," Sonny said.

"Let's just leave them," Sam said.

"Okay by me." I took a look around. The bones were now scattered around in a jumble — ribs here, leg bones over there, hand bones scattered, toe bones still in the shoes. The sight was causing me to take deep breaths. "What about the bones?"

Sonny shook his head. "Seems strange to me that nobody came out here and buried them. I don't care what he did, he ought to of got buried."

"Maybe they were too ashamed of themselves to come out here again and bury them," I said.

"Most likely," Sonny said.

None of us felt much like gathering those bones, however. "Maybe we could do it sometime," I said. "We'd need a couple of shovels and a pick."

"All right," Sam said. "Someday we'll do it." She looked at us. "Anything else we need to do here?"

There wasn't, so we got out of there.

I'd hardly left Sam off at her house when I began to feel that tightness and the little movements inside me. "Go away," I said. "You've got me into enough trouble."

"Don't say that, Gene. I came to congratulate you on your work. You're doing very well."

"I'm not doing it because you want me to. I've got my own reasons for it."

"That doesn't matter to me. What matters is

that you're beginning to see that your beloved grampa is not the sweet old man he's cracked up to be."

I was silent for a moment. I hated asking it for anything, but the voice knew a lot of things I wanted to know. So I said, "If you want me to do something for you, tell me what my dad had to do with it."

"You don't know much about your dad, do you, Gene?"

"No. They won't tell me."

"I'm not surprised. Talking about him would lead them onto dangerous subjects. Why is it fair for them to keep these things secret from you? He's your dad, isn't he?"

"You're keeping them secret from me, too. Why don't you tell me?"

"No, Gene. You won't believe me unless you find out for yourself."

"Suppose I don't want to find out. Suppose I decide to drop the whole thing."

"It isn't going to be so easy for you to make me go away."

"I'm tired of having you inside of me. Just tired of it."

It gave its low, throaty chuckle. "I expect you are. But I like it. It's pleasant for me to have somebody to talk to. Nice to have somebody to chat with from time to time."

I thought for a moment. "Those are your bones up there in the Toffey house, aren't they?"

"I wish people would stop calling it the Toffey house. Properly speaking, it's the Gallen house."

"Your house."

"I bought and paid for it."

"With money you swindled out of people."

"There you go again. Such an unpleasant term. They were grown-ups. They made their own choices. For a smart person, there's always money to be made from other people's greed."

I puzzled over that for a minute. "I don't get it."

"You will. Your beloved grampa could explain it to you, I'm sure." Then I felt the movements inside of me grow still, and the specter was gone.

Chapter 9

When I first thought about it, it seemed strange that my best friends and me would all have dads who were mixed up in this oil lynching. How come us? But by and by I realized that it wasn't so strange after all. A whole lot of people in Magnolia had got caught up in it. Got greedy for free money, the way Sonny had put it. A lot of kids around town were bound to have dads who'd been involved. So I decided it wasn't so strange that our three dads had been in on it.

Working together on it with Sonny and Sam made me feel a whole lot more comfortable than I had been. Still pretty scared a lot of the time. Still worried that the specter might find a way to make me go after Grampa. Still felt like I'd done something wrong for not having a dad, but it was a big help that we all liked each other. There wasn't any reason why we ought to like each other. Weren't on the same wavelength half the time. But we liked each other anyway. Maybe being on the same wavelength wasn't so important after all.

I was thinking about this as I got to our narrow little house and went in. Mom was in the kitchen. "Wash up for supper, Gene," she said. I went on upstairs to the little bathroom there and started washing my hands. I was still thinking about whether you had to be on the same wavelength as somebody to like them. Was I on the same wavelength as Grampa? Well, I don't guess a kid could ever exactly be on the same wavelength as a grown-up. They had too many different ideas about things. But partly you could. I mean, Grampa liked baseball and had played on the baseball team at the college he went to — he had a picture of his team lined up on bleacher seats wearing those funny old-fashioned baseball pants with high socks almost up to the knee.

Would I have been on the same wavelength

as my dad? Did he like baseball? Maybe right then he was reading in the evening paper about his favorite baseball team — Pittsburgh Pirates, New York Giants, Cleveland Indians, maybe. He could easily be living someplace like one of those. What if he sent me a railroad ticket to come and see him, saying he had box seats for the Detroit Tigers and I should hurry on up to Detroit and he'd meet me at the station and we'd go right out to the ball park to see Mickey Cochrane and Charlie Gehringer.

Suddenly I put my wet and soapy hands over my face and began to cry. It took me completely by surprise. I had no idea I was going to cry. I stood there with my wet and soapy hands over my face, the tears all mixed up with the soap, just crying away to beat the band and gasping for breath through the soap. Even while I was crying I was thinking what a strange thing I was doing, for I'd never cried over my dad before. It wasn't even so much something I was doing; it was more something that was happening to me. It hurt to think that he'd left me, but at the same time it was a relief to cry. And I figured maybe I ought to have cried about it sooner.

Mom knocked on the bathroom door. "You all right, Gene?"

I took a deep, shuddery breath. "I'm fine," I said. "I was washing my face and got soap in my eyes."

But right then I made my mind up about something. I went down to supper. Mom was putting the dishes on. Spanish rice, she called it—rice with tomatoes and a little hamburger mixed in for flavor. I waited until Mom had got us served and we'd started eating. Then I looked at them, one after the other. "You have to tell me about my dad. I have a right to know. You have to tell me."

Mom and Grampa looked at each other. "That's what's been bothering you, Gene?" Grampa said.

"Not just that. A lot of things."

Grampa nodded. "Tell us about it, Gene."

"No. You tell me about my dad."

Mom looked at Grampa. He put down his fork and leaned back in his chair for a minute. "Gene, I can certainly understand your feelings about it. It's perfectly normal for somebody in your position to want to know who his father is.

If it were me, I'd want to know, too." He paused to think. "Why has this come up all of a sudden?"

How was I going to answer that? "We found a news story in an old *Chronicle* that mentioned my dad. Thomas Richards. That's him, isn't it?" That much was true, anyway.

"Who's we?"

"Sonny, Sam, and me."

"What were you looking through old *Chronicle*s for?" Mom asked.

"Why are you grilling me?" I said. "I'm just trying to find out about my dad."

"We're not trying to grill you, Gene," Grampa said. "We just don't understand what this is all about. It's a little unusual for Sonny and Sam to be working on something together."

"You're not being fair," I said. "I'm just trying to find out about my dad and you keep changing the subject back to me. Something happened in Magnolia back then, something nobody ever talks about."

"Where'd you get that idea, Gene? From Alice Samuels? Can I suggest that Alice might be misinformed?"

"It isn't from Sam."

"Who, then?"

"I'm not going to tell you, Grampa. You won't tell me anything, why should I tell you anything? You're just beating around the bush."

"Yes, that's true. I'm being evasive. I have a reason for it. You're right. Something did happen in Magnolia back then. A number of people did some things they shouldn't have done. It's the opinion of those of us who know about it that it ought to be left where it lies. I can understand that you kids are curious, but I'd appreciate it very much if you'd drop the whole matter. You have plenty enough to keep you occupied. You don't need to go rummaging around in matters that are best left alone."

I looked square at him. "Grampa, did you do something you shouldn't have done back then?"

"Gene," Mom said, "I don't think you have a right to question your grandfather that way."

"Why not? He's questioning me."

"It's all right, May," Grampa said. "Yes, I made a mistake. An error of judgment. I've always been sorry for it, but it was an honest mistake. I made a decision and it turned out to have been the wrong one."

"My dad had something to do with it, didn't he?"

"Gene, I don't want to discuss this any further."

"I have a right to know about my dad."

He was silent for a minute. Then he said, "Someday, when you're older, we'll discuss the whole thing. Not now. It isn't anything a bunch of kids ought to be fooling around with. You're rushing into something you don't know anything about. People could be hurt." He picked up his fork. "That's all I'm going to say about it. I hope you kids will let the matter drop. Now let's eat the good supper your mom made for us while it's still hot."

They weren't going to tell me. I couldn't remember the last time I was sore at Grampa—probably sometime when I was little and he wouldn't let me play in the mud or something. But I was sore at him now. Sore at a lot of people, for that matter. Sore at Mom for siding with Grampa instead of me, sore at the specter for getting me into this mess, sore at the world, when you got down to it. So far as I could see, they were the ones who had done wrong, not me, but I was the one who was in trouble. About the only people I wasn't sore at were Sonny and Sam. They were sticking up for me. As far as I was concerned, everybody else could just disappear.

I guess I was sore at my dad, too, for not being there. I was beginning to see that probably he'd had to run for it back then. I hoped he'd been blamed for something he hadn't done. That would have made it easier for me to take. Why wasn't he here when I needed him? Was there any way I could get in touch with him? Find his phone number somehow? Or send him a message through the air? Maybe I could. I'd have to think about that.

After school on Monday we went over to the bandstand and I told them about it. Nice day, with the sun shining down through the big elms in the park in patches and pieces, a few big clouds, just the right kind of breeze. Perfect day for baseball, but I was too sore at the world for it. Too sore at the world for delivering groceries, too. The heck with them; they could carry their own groceries.

"I asked about the whole thing," I said.

"What happened back then, what my dad had done. They wouldn't tell me. Grampa said that if it came out, a lot of people would be hurt. He said he'd made a mistake back then. He claims it was an honest mistake, he was sorry about it, but he hadn't done it on purpose to hurt anyone."

"They wouldn't tell you about your dad, either?" Sam said.

"No."

"Don't you know where he lives? Couldn't you call him up?" she said.

"I don't think they know where he is. I don't think Mom wants to know where he is. She always says we should forget about him. But how can I forget about my own dad?"

"My mom wants us to forget about my dad, too," Sonny said. "She says we're better off without him. But sometimes at night when we're all in bed I hear her crying. Gene, maybe your mom cries in bed at night, too."

I had never thought about that side of it. "I don't think she would now," I said. "Maybe she did, once."

"We still haven't figured out what we're

going to do," Sam said. "If we knew exactly what happened back then, we might be able to figure out what the voice wants."

"It wants me to kill Grampa," I said.

"But why?" Sam said.

"Sam, your dad knows," I said. "Grampa knows. I'm pretty sure Sonny's dad knew."

"They all knew," Sonny said. "I don't see what's the big secret. Half the town must of known. Sam, did your dad ever say he'd heard a voice when he crashed into that tree?"

"He just said he blanked out for a minute. A mental lapse. He said it's a common enough thing."

"He didn't say nothing about hearing voices?"

"No. But I don't think he'd admit it even if he had. He's not the kind of person who would admit a thing like that."

"What if we asked him point-blank?" Sonny said.

Sam looked out through the park, then up in the sky, and then down to the ground. "I don't know if that's a good idea," she said.

"Why not?" Sonny said.

"I just don't think it's a good idea, Sonny."

"Sam, my grampa didn't like it very much when I asked him point-blank about my dad," I said. "But I did it anyway. We can't be scared of asking."

"I'm not scared," she said. "I only thought it wasn't a good idea."

"Gotta do it, Sam," Sonny said. "Gotta do it."

Sam gave Sonny a dirty look. "Did you ever ask your dad anything about it, Sonny?"

"Ask what? I didn't know nothing about a lynching until after he walked off that lumber platform. By then he wasn't in no kind of shape to ask anything of."

"You could have asked him about the oil certificates."

"Back then when I was little, it just seemed like some grown-up thing that wasn't of no interest to me."

"You could ask your mom."

"I did, a little while ago, before Dad died. I guess he knew he was in trouble, for he brought them oil certificates up again a couple of times. Told us we should take good care of them in case anything happened to him, because they might be worth a lot of money someday. He couldn't give up hoping. I was older, and more curious about such things. The next day, when Dad wasn't around, I asked her. She said she never understood what it was all about herself, except that it was some kind of bad business that it was best to stay away from. She didn't know, she said, and she didn't want to know." He paused. "So you see, Sam, I did my share of asking."

"Stop arguing about it," I said. "Sam, I brought it up with Grampa and Mom, so you've got to bring it up with your dad."

"All right," she said finally. "We'll all do it." We agreed we'd do it Sunday morning after church. Mr. Samuels put the paper to bed Saturday afternoon and generally took it easy on Sunday. So that was set.

The specter paid me a visit Friday afternoon when I was heading away from Snuffy's Groceries with a heavy box on my shoulder. "Go away," I said. "I'm busy. I don't want to talk to you when I've got a heavy box on my shoulder."

"You can put the box down for a minute, Gene. I'll be brief."

I kept on walking with the box on my shoulder. "I'm not listening," I said.

"This has been going on too long. We need to get moving. It's time we did something about Grampa."

"I told you, I'm not listening. You're just a swindler."

"I thought we weren't going to use that word. *Caveat emptor* is so much nicer. It's Latin, you know. It means 'let the buyer beware.'"

"I don't care what it means. I'm not listening."

"*Caveat emptor*. The spirit of American capitalism. A seller has a perfect right to present his wares in the best possible light."

"It wasn't in the spirit of anything. It was cheating, plain and simple. There was never any oil under that old Toffey farm and you knew it."

"Not so, Gene. There was never any evidence that there wasn't oil there. There might well have been. Nobody knew. Oil still might be found there."

I'd got suckered into arguing with him. "I told you, I'm not listening."

"They'll do anything they can to prove I was

wrong, but they can't prove it. A clever lawyer would have made the jury see that. I'd have gone scot-free. You know they're covering it up. That's as plain as the nose on one's face." He gave that throaty chuckle, like a heavy chain rattling. "A good deal plainer than the nose on my face, that's certain."

I didn't say anything, so the voice went on. "Gene, when you and your little friends broach this matter with Samuels on Sunday, you might ask him how they knew that the jail key was hidden in the first-aid kit."

This was interesting, and I forgot I wasn't listening. "Who knew?"

"It doesn't matter. I'll leave it at that. Just ask Samuels how they knew that the jail key was hidden in the first-aid kit."

"Who hid it there?"

"Remember, Gene, I'm growing impatient. I'm not going to wait much longer. It's time we got cracking on this. Catch him alone. Use a baseball bat. Nobody will suspect anything if you're seen carrying a baseball bat around. There won't be much blood. Rifle his pockets afterwards, take his money, your mom's rings.

The police will think it was a robbery. You came in from baseball and found him sprawled on the floor. Nobody will ever suspect you."

I shuddered. "No!" I shouted. "Never. Now go away."

"Soon, Gene," the voice said. "Soon."

Sonny and I went over to Sam's house after church—after church for Sam, anyway. Mom had a rush typing job to do that had to be ready Monday morning, so we hadn't gone, and Sonny had hardly been inside a church in his life.

He'd hardly been inside a house like the Samuels', either. The Samuels weren't rich by any means, but they were comfortable. Mr. Samuels said he probably could have made more money if he'd stayed on the *St. Louis Post-Dispatch*. He'd won a couple of prizes for his stories, and would have been an editor there by now, but he liked running his own show. Money wasn't the key thing, he always said; it was doing the kind of work you wanted to do.

We came in through the front door and Sonny stood there looking around. He wasn't in awe, nothing like that, just curious about how people like the Samuels lived. Sofa, a couple of bookcases with glass doors, framed prizes Mr. Samuels had won hanging on the walls, window curtains pulled back, little plaster statuettes of shepherds and shepherdesses dancing on top of the bookcases, a piano, a big carpet with a shiny floor showing around the edges, on the piano a silver dish of mints we weren't supposed to hook but always did.

The windows in Sonny's cabin had never seen a curtain, the only books were his dad's cowboy magazines, and I doubt if he knew the difference between a mint and an aspirin, for he'd probably never eaten either one.

Sam came downstairs from her room when she heard us come in. "Did he say he'd talk to us?" I asked.

"He knows we're onto something. I don't know how he figured it out. Maybe I said something wrong."

"We're gonna tell him anyway," Sonny said. "It don't matter if he figured it out."

"He's out in the sunroom," Sam said. We hooked a couple of mints from the silver dish on the piano and went on out there. Sun coming in, red and yellow Mexican rug on the floor, more bookcases, some ferns in a big pot, a painting of some cathedral, another painting of cowboys in a water hole fighting off some Indians. Mr. Samuels was lying on a sofa, his leg in a cast, writing on a yellow lined pad. He was a big guy, not fat, but a little flabby. "Hello, kids," he said. He'd known me pretty much all my life and he knew at least who Sonny was, knew his dad. A newspaperman like him gets to know a lot of people around town. He put the yellow lined pad on the floor. "Sonny, I'm sorry about your dad. I can't say I knew him well, but I knew him a little. I never took against him. I don't see where he ever harmed anyone but himself."

"Yes, sir," Sonny said.

"What's on your minds, kids?"

Sonny and I looked at Sam. "Dad." She took a quick look at Sonny and me. She was pretty nervous about this, even though it was her own dad. "Dad, we're finding out about something that happened in Magnolia a while back that nobody ever talks about."

"Oh?" he said. He cocked his head to one side and looked us over. "And what is that?"

"Somebody was lynched," she said.

He kind of gave a jerk and stared at us. Then he relaxed again. "Where'd you get that idea, kids?"

We looked at one another. We could see that we ought to have worked out a story first. I figured it was safest to come as close to the truth as we could. "Mr. Samuels, when we were going through the *Chronicle*s we saw something about there being oil under the old Toffey house. It made some mention of my dad. Tom Richards. I got curious about it. There wasn't anything wrong with that, was there?"

"No, Gene, nothing wrong with it. It's perfectly natural that you'd want to know about your father. Of course I knew him. I can't say I knew him very well, but enough to chat with when I ran into him. But if you're going to ask me about him, it isn't up to me to tell you. That's your mom's business. She and your grampa."

"They won't tell me anything. I didn't think you'd tell me anything, either. That isn't why we came."

He looked from one of us to the next. "Why'd you come, then?"

"We want to know about the lynching, Dad," Sam said. "Half the people in town were involved. Sonny thinks his dad was in on it somehow, Gene's dad, his grampa." She took a deep breath. "You knew about it and kept it out of the paper."

He gave a little smile. "Now hold it, kids. You're letting your imaginations run away with you. Who said there was a lynching?"

"We know it," Sonny said. "There was a lynching, all right."

"How are you so sure, Sonny?"

"Dad, we went out to the Toffey house. Nobody ever goes out there. Sonny's dad told him it was a good place to stay away from. We got curious and we went there."

"Oh? And what did you find?"

Once again we looked at one another to see whose turn it was to speak. "We found a noose," Sam said. "And underneath, a heap of bones and half-rotted clothes."

Mr. Samuels didn't say anything for a bit, but sat there with the white cast sticking out in front of him, thinking. "Did you find anything else? That's it? The bones and the clothes?"

"We found this, Dad," Sam said. She held out the clipping from the newspaper.

Mr. Samuels took it and scanned it quickly. Then he handed it back to Sam. "Where did you find it?"

"In the dead guy's pocket," Sonny said.

Mr. Samuels nodded his head. "Well, I can understand your curiosity, kids. You're all bright, imaginative kids and something like this would excite your interest. Bound to. But I think you're adding up two and two to make twenty-two. That old Toffey house has been a nuisance for years. It's always attracted people we'd just as soon not see around Magnolia. People down on their luck, traveling between St. Louis and Kansas City. Bums, not to put too fine a point on it. You can feel sorry for them, but unfortunately they'll steal anything that isn't nailed down. They pass the word among themselves that the old Toffey house is a place where they can sleep when they're passing through. It wouldn't be surprising that one of those fellows had died out there. Got drunk, fell asleep in cold weather, and froze to death. It happens all the time. Killed in a fight. Or simply had a heart attack. Any number of things could have happened."

"That doesn't explain the noose," I said.

He shrugged again. "They could have no relationship, the one to the other. Somebody could have put the noose up as a macabre joke after they stumbled across the body. Or it was put up at some time to warn people off."

"It seems like too much of a coincidence, Dad," Sam said.

"Yes, it probably does," he said. "Could have been a lynching, a case where two or three bums were sleeping out there. Caught one of them stealing; they were drinking and decided to lynch the thief. That happens, too." He shook his head. "I'm sorry to spoil your fun, kids. A lynching would be a lot more interesting than a quarrel among bums, but I've been in the newspaper business long enough to see a thousand interesting stories melt away under a cold look."

"What about the oil swindle?" Sonny asked. "My dad had oil certificates out of it. My mom's still got them. She says she ought to throw them away, but they were something Dad saved for years and she can't bring herself to just toss them out."

"Look, kids, that's an ancient story. I don't remember exactly what it was about anymore myself. It's long forgotten around Magnolia."

"Dad," Sam said. "How come you never ran anything in the *Chronicle* about it?"

"What makes you think I didn't?"

"Mr. Samuels," I said, "we went through all the *Chronicle*s for that time and we didn't see anything. A story like that must have been pretty big for a little town like Magnolia. It should have been on the front page."

He looked from one of us to the other. "There never was any school project, was there, kids? You made that story up as an excuse to examine the back issues, didn't you?"

We didn't say anything.

"I thought so," he said. "What's this all about? Who put you up to it?"

Once again we looked at one another, wondering what to tell him. Why hadn't we worked out a story before? "We got it from my dad," Sonny said. "He was being haunted by some voice. That's why he stepped off the lumber platform. The voice told him to do it."

"Sonny, I don't mean to be disrespectful of the dead, but how could he have told you this when he was already dead himself?"

"He told us before. Me and Mom. She can tell you. He was being haunted by a voice that was always telling him to jump in front of cars and such."

"He was hearing voices in his head?"

"A voice. He wasn't making it up. It was really happening to him. It was the specter of the man who got lynched."

Mr. Samuels nodded his head. "I see. That makes things a little clearer. Sonny, I know that your dad had his problems. That's no secret around town. No offense meant—a lot of people have problems, some of them a great deal worse than his. I didn't know that it had gotten so bad that he was hearing voices in his head. It makes what he did a little more understandable. I feel sorry for him. He must have been suffering a good deal. But we can't allow ourselves to take as fact the ramblings of a person with mental problems."

"Dad wasn't having mental problems," Sonny said. "He was being haunted."

Mr. Samuels looked annoyed. "Sonny, I respect your loyalty to your father. That's creditable in you. But—"

"Dad, it's real," Sam said. "Gene—"

"Look, kids, I've got work to do." He was getting sore. "The paper still has to come out, broken leg or no broken leg. You're letting your imaginations run away with you. There are no such things as ghosts, specters, whatever you want to call them."

There was a moment of silence. Then I said, "How did the lynch mob know that the jail key was in the first-aid kit?"

The room was suddenly dead quiet. Mr. Samuels swung his leg off the sofa and sat up. He looked at us for a moment. Then he said softly, "How'd you know about that, Gene?"

"The specter told me, the same as it told Sonny's dad to walk off into midair." I paused. "The same as it told you to drive into that tree."

"That was a mental lapse," he said.

"No, it wasn't," Sonny said. "The specter was trying to kill you the same as it killed my dad."

Mr. Samuels turned his head to look out the window at the sun shining on the maple tree in the side yard. Finally he turned back to us and shook his head. "I suppose we were wrong to think that we could bury this thing forever. You kids are right. There was a lynching in Magnolia. This fellow Gallen, it was. He'd been swindling people with this oil deal. Some of us had been suspicious from the start, but a lot of people around here smelled easy money and got suckered. People were throwing their lifetime savings at Gallen. Finally some of us realized it had to be stopped. We called in the FBI and the thing quickly collapsed. We jailed Gallen, but at three o'clock in the morning some fellows came out to the jail. We didn't have but two cells then. We never had any need for any more, never had any real criminals around here. Locked up drunks who got to fighting from time to time. Mostly the cells stood empty.

"I don't know where Gene got it from, but he's right. The key was hidden in the first-aid kit. They had different hiding places for it, but it was there that night. Only three or four people knew about it. The fire chief, in case the jail caught on fire, the two constables—that was all the police force we had at the time. The mayor, I guess. One of them revealed the hiding place to the mob. I don't know who, and don't want to know. The mob came to the jail, ran the constable on duty out of there, found the key. They took this poor fellow Gallen out to the old Toffey place and hung him. It was a terrible thing for them to do. But there were some good people involved in it who got caught up in the emotions of the moment. Family men, good citizens who took care of their own. Those of us who knew about it decided it was best for the town to forget about it. Let the waters close over it. We put out the word that the prisoner had been transferred to another jurisdiction for trial."

We were silent. Then Sam said, "Dad, why didn't somebody go out there and bury those bones?"

"At first we didn't know they were there. We knew that Gallen had been taken out of jail, but we didn't know where they'd taken him. Then, a few years later a rumor began to go around. Somebody had a little too much to drink and said something in a bar. We talked about it—John

Adamson, myself, the fellow who was mayor at the time. We saw that we were stuck. Disposing of those bones without reporting them to the police was about as illegal as you can get. If we'd got caught it would have meant real trouble. Not just to us: there'd have been an investigation, and like as not the whole story would have come out. The men who'd lynched Gallen would have faced long jail sentences, maybe even the electric chair. An awful lot of people would have been hurt. Not just the men, but their wives, children, parents, friends. Half the town, near enough. We decided to leave well enough alone. Let time pass."

"Mr. Samuels," I said, "weren't you afraid somebody might stumble on the bones by chance?"

"Oh, sure. That was the risk we had to take. But since the Depression there are a lot of abandoned farmhouses around here. Farmers couldn't pay their mortgages, lost their farms, went out to California to work picking fruit and such. One more abandoned farmhouse wouldn't attract special attention. We decided to take the risk. And it worked, until now."

We were all quiet for a little bit. Then Sonny said, "My dad was one of them who started it."

Mr. Samuels shook his head. "I'm not going to say anything more about it. What's done is done. I'm going to ask you kids to forget about the whole thing. I've leveled with you. I've told you what you wanted to know. You owe me something. I want you to drop it."

"Mr. Samuels," I said. "How come they didn't lynch my dad? How did he get away?"

Mr. Samuels thought for a minute. "You're concerned that your dad might have been involved in something criminal, aren't you, Gene?"

"I guess so," I said.

He considered for another minute. "Well, it isn't my business to tell you about your father. That's up to your mom and your grampa. But I guess there's no harm in telling you that Tom — your dad — was mighty proud of you, the way any young father would be proud to have a fine, healthy baby boy." He glanced at Sam. "Nothing wrong with having a baby girl, either, but Tom was proud he'd got a boy. I remember, Sunday mornings he'd carry you out to the

Magnolia Diner for breakfast so your mom could sleep late. I'd go out for the Sunday papers about that time, and I'd see him through the diner window. He'd have you kneeling up in the booth next to him so he could feed you bites of sausage and pancakes. I don't imagine that sausages and pancakes were the best breakfast for a little tot, but it didn't seem to do you any harm." He paused again. "I—that's about as much as I ought to say. You can ask your mom about him."

He leaned back on the sofa. "Look, I have an editorial to write. I have to get to work. Now, I want you to forget about this ghost business — specter, whatever you call it. Yes, I understand that people sometimes think they're hearing things. It happens to everybody—a little voice at the back of your head saying something odd. I know it seems real at the time. But it's imaginary. Sometimes the mind plays tricks on itself. I want you to forget about that stuff."

The only trouble was that the specter wasn't going to let us forget about it.

Chapter 10

"You see, Gene, I was right," the hollow voice said. "They lynched me, and Samuels and your grampa covered it up. Covered up a murder, Gene. Let the men who killed me go free. Do you think that's right, Gene?"

I was up in my room, studying for an English test. What with everything that had been happening, I was pretty far behind in stuff I was supposed to be reading. "Okay, you were right. I admit it. Why can't you just forget about it? You deserved it, swindling all those people out of their savings."

"Nobody deserves to be murdered, Gene. With a good lawyer I'd have got off, anyway. Found not guilty. Found innocent of all charges."

I was determined not to let him see I was scared. "How could you be innocent? There was no oil under that land and you knew it."

"They'd have had to prove I knew there was no oil on the place. That's a hard thing to prove, Gene. In this America you're innocent until proven guilty."

"I don't care what they could prove or couldn't prove. You were guilty. You deserved it."

"Think of it, Gene. Think what it means to be waked up suddenly at three in the morning by a bunch of men with paper bags over their heads. Big eyeholes cut into the paper bags. Oh, those eyeholes staring at you, black spots staring. They grab you, half awake, stuff a handkerchief in your mouth so you can't shout. You're choking, and they tie your hands behind you, tie your feet together, handle you rough. I tried to fight, but I didn't have a chance, not against a dozen men punching and pulling at me. They carried me out of there, tossed me in the back of a truck, and off we went with three men crouched over me holding rifles. Out to the Toffey place. My place. I never bothered to furnish it. Old farms weren't my cup of tea.

Elegant hotels with marble lobbies and palm trees were more my style.

"Of course, they took me out there because they knew nobody would be around. A half mile down to the end of that road, where nobody ever went. Think of it, Gene. Scared to death and fighting like mad even if it was no use, knowing that in five or ten minutes I'd be dangling in the air, the breath choking out of me.

"They put the noose around my neck, ran the rope up through that light fixture. Four men grabbed the rope and pulled me up by the neck until I was two feet off the ground, jerking around, trying to shout, gasping for air. Then they left. I can't say how long I dangled there, struggling and gasping. Seemed like forever at the time, but I don't guess it was more than five minutes at most. A person can't go without air for very long."

I had been a little child back in 1925 when the specter was lynched. What had I thought when I got up in the morning and my dad was gone—just gone, no explanation, disappeared for good into thin air? No more Sunday breakfasts kneeling up beside him in the booth in the diner, being fed bits of sausage and pancakes soaked in maple syrup. No more whatever else we did together. No nothing anymore.

I didn't remember any of it—didn't remember the pancakes and sausages, didn't remember what he looked like, what it felt like to snuggle down beside him in the diner, smelling the sausages, smelling his aftershave, if he wore any. Didn't remember any of it. I wished I did. I wished I could remember kneeling in that booth next to my dad, holding a fork in my fist and stabbing around at the plate to get hold of a piece of pancake. It would have meant a lot to me to remember that. But I couldn't. "Tell me what happened to my dad."

"Yes, you'd want to know that, wouldn't you? They let him go, of course. They shouldn't have, but naturally they did. He was a local man, upstanding family man, married to the judge's daughter. Of course they let him go. I was from Chicago, and they didn't let me go."

"Who let him go?"

"You'll have to ask your beloved grampa about that. He knows."

"Do you know where my dad is now?"

"Yes, Gene. Perhaps, if things work out the way I want them to, I could tell you where he is."

"You mean if I kill Grampa for you." I could feel myself tighten and grow cold.

"You have a chance to redress the wrong that was done to me, Gene. You're a fair-minded boy. You can even the score. It's only right, Gene. You must be able to see that."

"No, I don't," I said. "I don't see where killing somebody else does you any good now. What good will it do you?"

"Ah, you don't understand, Gene. I might find peace at last."

I considered. "What had Grampa to do with it? He would never have gone out with a mob and lynched somebody."

"He might as well have. It came down to the same thing in the end."

"Well, you can forget about it. I'm not going to do it. Now, leave me alone. I have to finish reading my book."

"Oh, but you're going to do it, Gene. Very soon. In the next few days. You're going to take a baseball bat and crack it across his skull. I've seen you swing a baseball bat, Gene. I've seen you hit a ball down the third baseline so hard it handcuffed the fielder."

There was no use pretending I wasn't scared. He'd made Sonny's dad walk off into midair; he'd made Mr. Samuels drive into a tree. "I won't do it," I said. My voice was cracked and ragged.

"Yes, you will, Gene. There's no use fighting me. You might as well accept it." Then it was gone.

I wished I could tell Grampa about all of this. There was no way I could walk up to him and say, "Grampa, you better watch out, because I might try to kill you." No way I could get him to understand that the specter was real, that it had already killed somebody and was likely to kill somebody else. I figured my dad would believe me. He'd know. He was bound to, considering everything. He'd believe me if I told him about the specter. Why couldn't I tell him? Why had he run away and left me facing the voice by myself? I whispered, "Come back, Dad. Come back. I need you. I really need you."

But there was no answer. I had to tell Grampa something. I had to talk to him. I had to at least find out what he'd done wrong to get the specter so angry at him. Maybe it would turn out that Grampa had a good explanation for what happened that would satisfy the specter. I wasn't going to bet on that, but it was worth a try.

I had something else to do first, however. My baseball bat was a thirty-two-inch Reach that Grampa had given me for my birthday a couple of years back. He'd taken me to Brown's Sporting Goods on Water Street so I could pick out a bat that suited me. He'd advised me to get the biggest bat I could manage, because I was getting my growth spurt and would grow into it soon enough. It was just about perfect for me now.

After supper I got it out of my room, where I kept it leaning in a corner. Then I walked with it over to Sonny's cabin. Sonny was sitting on the car seat on the porch in the twilight, eating a pork sandwich and reading one of his dad's cowboy magazines. They didn't eat at regular times at the Hawkins'. I sat down beside him on the car seat. "How can you read in the dark, Sonny?"

"It ain't that dark. I can read when there ain't hardly any light. I'm reading this here *West*

magazine. Pretty good stuff. They got this char-
acter called Stoney Lonesome, who's big and
strong but gentle with everybody 'cept crooks.
You can't help liking him. I wouldn't mind being
strong and gentle like him."

"You told me once you'd never seen a grown-
up you wanted to be like."

"Stoney Lonesome ain't a grown-up. He's in
a book," Sonny said. "They got a lotta stories
about him in Dad's cowboy magazines."

"What're you going to do when you've read
your dad's magazines all up? You'll have to start
buying your own."

"Naw, *Yew*gene, I wouldn't waste the money.
I'll just read 'em all over again. Half of 'em are
pretty much the same anyway."

"You know, Sonny, you can get cowboy
books from the library for free. They have a lot
of them there."

"I wouldn't go to no library. It ain't my style.
The library might be all right for you and Sam,
but it don't suit me. Too much like a church."

"It isn't like a church, Sonny," I said. "It's different, except that you have to be quiet."

"Maybe that's it. I don't like having to be

quiet. Makes me feel closed in. To tell the truth, *Yew*gene, most every kind of rule makes me feel closed in. Expect I got it from my dad. He didn't like having no job, for it made him feel closed in. I reckon having a wife and kids made him feel closed in, too. I've said he shouldn't of had us, but where would that have left me?"

"You have to get over feeling closed in by everything, Sonny. It won't do you any good."

He decided to change the subject. "What you got your bat for, *Yew*gene? Getting a little dark for baseball."

"The specter was on me again. About Grampa. He says he wants me to do it soon. I'm scared half to death I might do it."

"What's the bat got to do with it?" Sonny said.

"He wants me to use the bat to—for it. It won't seem strange for me to come walking in with a bat. Says I should catch Grampa alone and make it look like robbers did it. He says nobody'll suspect me."

"Probably they wouldn't," Sonny said. "Probably you could get away with it."

"I don't care about that. If I ever did it I'd

have to kill myself anyway. Jump out of a window or something. I couldn't live with myself."

Sonny took a bite of his sandwich and nodded. "I can see that," he said. "I don't know as I could live with myself neither if I killed my grampa. Wouldn't matter so much if it was one of my twerpy sisters." He paused to chew. "Of course, I ain't got any grampa. So far as I know. Mom's dad died a while back and Dad's father wouldn't speak to him."

"I figured it might be a good idea for me to leave my bat at your house."

"You really think you might do it, Gene?"

"It worries the pants off me, Sonny. Look what the specter did to your dad. Look what it did to Sam's dad. If your dad couldn't fight it off, how do you think I'm going to?"

"Well, I don't know," he said. "We got to think of something."

But we couldn't think of anything. "I better get home," I said. "I've got to see if I can find out some more from Grampa." I handed Sonny the bat. "If I come around wanting it back and acting funny, don't give it to me."

"I won't, Gene. You can bet on that."

I went on home. Grampa was sitting in his easy chair by the front window, listening to the news on the radio. The announcer was saying that the Senate would probably approve the new Social Security program that President Roosevelt wanted to put in. I didn't know what Social Security was and didn't care. "Where's Mom, Grampa?"

"She went to her church meeting. She said she'd be back by nine."

I reached over and turned the radio off.

"Hey, Gene," Grampa said. "I want to hear the news. This Social Security bill is important."

"I don't care," I said. "I have to talk to you. You have to tell me some things." I didn't sit down, but stood in front of him so he wouldn't be above me.

He saw that I was serious. "All right," he said. "I can read about the Social Security bill in the paper tomorrow. What's on your mind?"

I crossed my arms over my chest. "We found out what happened in Magnolia a while back."

"Oh? What did you discover?"

"Somebody was lynched out at the old Toffey house. Somebody who was involved in an oil swindle."

He stared at me for a moment, his mouth puffed out. "What makes you think that?"

"We went out there."

"You, Sonny, and Sam, I assume."

"Yes."

"And?"

"We found a noose hanging from a light fixture in an upstairs room. And under the noose a body. Well, the bones of a body. The rest of him had rotted away."

His mouth was tight. "Why on earth were you kids prowling around up there?"

For a moment I thought about telling him about the voice. But he'd never believe me. Instead, I said, "We saw some stuff in one of the old *Chronicle*s about an oil swindle. It mentioned the old Toffey house."

"Yes. Go on."

"It also mentioned my dad. Thomas Richards. That was him, wasn't it?"

He nodded his head. "It was."

"Sonny figured out his dad was involved, because he owned these oil certificates he kept in an envelope in his bureau. Sam figured her dad had something to do with it, because he didn't run anything about it in the paper. Nothing about a lynching at all. We saw that all our fathers were mixed up in it, so we went on out there and discovered the dead guy."

"Hold it a minute, Gene. There's a piece missing here. What made you conclude that somebody had been lynched if there was nothing about it in the *Chronicle*?"

I could have made it clearer to him if I'd been able to tell him about the specter. "We found a newspaper clipping from the St. Louis paper about it."

"Found it where?"

"Out at the Toffey house," I said. "It was in the dead man's pocket." I paused. "Grampa, Mr. Samuels admitted the whole thing."

He jerked his head back in surprise. "Samuels told you about this?"

"He had to. We'd figured out most of it already. This Gallen guy had come out from Chicago, bought the old Toffey house, and told everybody there was oil under it. He got caught, and they lynched him." I paused again. "What I want to know is what you did. You helped to cover it up, didn't you?"

He leaned back in his chair with his hands behind his head and looked up at the ceiling. Then he sighed. "I suppose we were foolish to think we could keep it a secret forever. Too many people knew about it." He looked back at me. "But I'll tell you, Gene, bringing it all out is going to make a lot of trouble for people around here. Sonny, for example. Does he really want people to know what his dad did back then?"

"Sonny knows. He doesn't know exactly what his dad did, but he knows it wasn't right."

He took his hands from behind his head and nodded. "I suppose Sam knows that her dad was part of the cover-up, as you put it."

"Yes. We figured that out. She didn't want to believe it at first, but her dad confessed."

He nodded. "Yes, we covered it up. That's true, Gene. We thought that it was best for everybody in town to let the waters close over it. I still think so. I thought it was the right decision. You have to remember, Gene, that if we'd brought in the state prosecutor there'd have been an investigation and these men might have gone to jail for murder. Family men, a lot of them, who'd walked straight all their lives but got caught up in the emotions of this."

"Is that what you did that was wrong?"

He gave me a funny look. "Gene, why do you keep insisting that I did something wrong back then?"

"Because—" But I couldn't tell him how I knew. "Sonny said his dad told him."

He nodded. "All right. I'll tell you about it. I'm not ashamed. It was a mistake, but it was an honest mistake. You see, Gene, right from the beginning some of us were suspicious of the whole thing. It didn't make sense that nobody had ever figured out there was oil around here before. At the time people all over the United States were running around looking for oil in hopes of getting rich. Somebody was bound to have tested the area around here. So I checked with somebody I knew in the geology department at Washington University in St. Louis. They told me that a survey of the area had been done some years back, and there wasn't much chance of finding oil around here.

"But people in Magnolia were throwing money at this fellow Gallen—throwing their life's savings at him, anything they could lay their hands on."

"Sonny's dad sold his car and his fishing boat to get money to invest in it."

He nodded. "He wasn't the only one. Gene, you take a fellow who's never had anything and never expects to have anything. A fellow who has been looking up from the bottom of the barrel all his life, working hard jobs since he was fourteen years old, and knows he'll go on working hard jobs until the day he dies, because he hasn't got any pension—nothing like the Social Security that Roosevelt wants to put in. Knows he can't possibly save enough to carry him in his old age. Suddenly he sees a chance to raise himself up a little, walk around town with some cash in his pocket, buy a little car, get his wife a couple of new dresses, bicycles for the kids. It doesn't take much to persuade a person wearing those shoes to spend what little he's saved to buy a piece of pie in the sky.

"I was a judge, I had contacts with the prosecutor's office in St. Louis. They got in touch with the FBI. It didn't take them long to get the goods on the fellow. He was known—had run similar swindles in other places. They picked him up and jailed him here. They jailed your poor dad along with him because he was Gallen's partner. They were brought before me to set bail. I figured your dad wouldn't run. He could make a case that he'd been victimized by Gallen along with everybody else, and maybe get off with a short sentence. Maybe get off scot-free. Besides, he had a wife and a child in Magnolia whom he adored and wasn't likely to flee. So I set a reasonable bail for him, and let him go home.

"But I knew I couldn't turn Gallen loose. He'd disappear as quick as lightning. He begged and pleaded. He said that the whole town was against him, and that his life wouldn't be worth two cents if I held him in jail. He'd gotten death threats, anonymous letters."

He frowned and rubbed his forehead. "That's where I made my mistake. I should have taken the death threats more seriously. You understand, Gene, that death threats of that kind are pretty common. Every judge gets them once in a while from people he's sent to jail. So I discounted the death threats. What I should have done was to transfer Gallen to another town where they had better security than our two constables. I didn't, and at three in the morning some masked men came, took Gallen away, and hanged him."

I didn't say anything for a minute, but stood staring at Grampa. Then I said, "Do you know who they were?"

He nodded. "Pretty much. It's hard to keep a thing like that quiet. People hear a neighbor's car start at three in the morning. A wife wakes up and discovers that her husband isn't there. Somebody with a couple of drinks under his belt starts dropping little hints. It gets around."

"Was Mr. Hawkins one of them?"

"That's what I always heard. Mind you, Gene, I don't have any evidence." He rubbed his forehead again. "You have to understand that people were bitterly angry. They were seeing their life's savings going down the drain. Losing their houses in some cases. I didn't understand that well enough. But your dad did. For several days they'd been coming to him asking where their money was. He was the front man, the spokesman for the operation. Gallen was spending a lot of time in Chicago, I gather, and your dad had to deal with all these angry people. Gallen was clever that way. He wanted to have somebody out front to take the heat. So it was your dad who was seeing the bitterness in people's faces, hearing the anger in their voices. He knew there was a good chance they'd turn violent. Knew it better than I did. So the minute I turned him loose he took what little money he had and disappeared. Drove off into the night."

I stood thinking for a minute. There was something else I wanted to know, but was afraid of getting an answer I wouldn't like. I took a deep breath. "Grampa, did Dad know it was a swindle—know there wasn't any oil under the Toffey farm?"

Grampa shrugged. "Gene, people can get themselves to believe whatever they want to believe. I can only guess, but I suppose way down inside where he didn't have to notice it, he must have known there was something suspicious about it. But he didn't have to believe that. Gallen said he had an expert's opinion that there was oil there. Your dad had no particular reason to disbelieve that, and so he didn't." Grampa shrugged again. "But I'm only guessing about that, Gene."

"Do you think it was wrong for him to run away?"

He didn't say anything for a minute. Then he said, "He must have known that he was finished in Magnolia. He'd never be able to have a life here. Wouldn't be able to find a job, wouldn't have any friends. He'd have been ostracized. You and your mom, too. And of course he knew there was a chance he could have gotten what poor Gallen got. So he left."

"Why didn't he take us with him?"

Grampa shrugged. "You'll have to ask your mom about that."

Then the front door opened, and Mom came in. "You two look mighty serious," she said. "What have you been talking about?"

"Oh, various things," Grampa said. "How was your meeting?"

"Boring as usual. Old Mrs. Saunders never knows when to shut up." She looked at me. "Gene, just before I went out somebody phoned you."

"Who? Sam?"

"No, it wasn't. It was some man. I asked him who it was, but he wouldn't tell me. It seemed a little strange to me."

"It was my dad."

"Now, Gene," she said. She gave me a little smile. "It was not your dad. Probably somebody looking for a boy to do some work and heard of you."

I was sure of it. "It was my dad."

"Gene," Grampa said. "I know your dad has been on your mind a good deal lately. No doubt because of the matters we've just been talking about. That's understandable. But you have to be realistic. After all this time it's very unlikely that your dad would try to get in touch with you."

"It was my dad. I know it."

"How can you be so sure, Gene?" Mom said.

"I'm sure. Did it sound like my dad, Mom?"

"I haven't heard him speak for years, Gene. I hardly remember. Now really, you have to get over this idea."

"But he sounded like my dad."

"Gene, many people sound the same on the telephone. You can't go by that. You've got to let it go. It's very unlikely we'll ever hear anything from him again."

"I suggest we drop all of this for one evening," Grampa said. "I want to see if I can get any news about the Social Security bill."

But I knew it was my dad. Maybe he'd call again if I asked him.

Chapter 11

I was scared of playing baseball—scared of holding a baseball bat in my hands. I didn't really see how the specter could make me kill Grampa, but I was afraid that he could. I felt confused, not really able to think clearly about anything, and I wondered if the specter was causing that, too.

He caught me the next afternoon after school.

"Can't you leave me alone for a little while? I'm just sick of all of this."

"I'm sorry, Gene. It'll be over soon. We're going to do it very soon. Sooner than you think."

"No. I'm not going to do it. Ever."

"Yes, Gene. Yes you are. Very soon."

"No. Go away. No, never."

"I'll go away when it's done, Gene. I'll go away when your grampa is sprawled on the floor with a crack in his skull."

"No," I shouted. "No, no, no. You can't make me."

"Yes, I can, Gene. And I will." And it was gone.

I felt weak and scared, for the voice was coming for me, and I didn't know if I could fight it off. When would it come? Soon, it said. Today? Tomorrow? The next day? No longer than that. Could I fight it off? I didn't know.

I felt too scared to go to Snuffy's, so I went on home. Mom was in the kitchen ironing one of Grampa's shirts. "Where's Grampa?" I asked.

"He went over to the *Chronicle* office to see Mr. Samuels. He had to talk to him about something."

"Did that guy say he'd phone me again?"

"No," Mom said. She looked at me. "Gene, you have to forget about your dad. When you're a grown-up you'll be free to do what you want about him. I won't be able to stop you."

"Do you think I'll be able to find him then?"

"Often you can in these cases. There are people who make a business of tracing lost persons. It's expensive, but often they can find the person."

"Why don't you want to see him, Mom?"

"I just don't, is all," she said firmly. "I think we're better off as we are, Gene. Someday you'll understand. I hope you will, anyway. Now, let's drop the subject."

I went upstairs to my room, but instead of doing my homework like I should have, I sat on my bed with my hands over my face. "Dad," I whispered. "I need you. I need you now, right away. The specter is after me. It's going to make me do something terrible. Please, Dad. I need you. Please call me again. I'm sorry I wasn't home before. I'm home now. I'll wait. Please call."

I sat on the bed and waited. Nothing happened. I waited some more. Still nothing, so I went to my table, took out my math book, and began working on some problems—tried to, anyway, but I didn't have much heart for it.

Fifteen minutes later I heard the phone ring downstairs. I jumped up, ran out of the room, and clattered downstairs. Grampa was on the phone by the living room table. "Right," he said. "Sure. Thanks. Good-bye."

"That wasn't my dad, was it?"

"No. It was Mr. Samuels. As you can imagine, we've been talking. You kids have raised a lot of problems we're trying to head off."

"Grampa, if my dad called, would you let me talk to him?"

"Yes. I would. I don't think your mom would."

"Where is she?"

"She went over to Mrs. Saunders' to discuss the church supper. She said she wouldn't be gone long."

"Grampa, why won't Mom tell me about my dad?"

He gazed at me for a while, and then he went back to his easy chair by the window and sat down. "She's stubborn. Your dad let her down, and she hasn't found it easy to forgive him." He thought for a minute. "Gene, you're not doing yourself any good by brooding over this. You need to forget about him."

"Mom said that when I grew up I might be able to find him."

He nodded. "It's quite possible. You never know about these things."

"Will you tell me what he was like?"

He thought some more. "It might take some of the mystery out of it for you to know. Don't tell your mom. This will have to be between you and me."

"Yes. I understand."

He nodded again. "He was a decent enough fellow, Gene. That much I can say for him. He came out of St. Louis to work as assistant manager at the Magnolia Hotel when new owners came in. They brought him out. Had big plans for him. He was young, good-looking, had good manners, a nice way of talking. Gift of gab, as they say. He was well liked around town. Your mom fell for him. A lot of the girls around here did. Your mom was good-looking, too—still is, if I say so myself, although she's my daughter. She was popular, and they hit it off, the two of them.

"To be honest, Gene, I had my doubts about him from the start. He struck me as a good-hearted fellow, but weak. More interested in having a good time than in getting on with the job—liked to have a laugh, a drink with the fellows. But your mom was smitten, and I knew if I tried to stand in her way she'd marry him anyway. So they got married, and a year or so later you came along. Not long after that your dad lost his job at the Magnolia Hotel. I never quite knew the truth of it. The accounts were a muddle, and a good deal of money was missing. I don't believe your dad took the money. He wasn't dishonest. It was more likely that he was living a little too high on the hotel's money — taking people to dinner, giving them tickets to Broadway shows when they came through St. Louis, that sort of thing. He saw it as good publicity for the hotel, I'm sure, but I've also no doubt that he substantially overdid it, without really meaning to. You know how it is. In the weakness of the moment he'd pick up the dinner check for a party of people and charge it to the hotel. Wanted to look like a big shot, I suppose.

"Well, it doesn't matter now. But of course rumors went around, and people were leery of hiring him. So he set himself up in the used car business. I lent him some money to get started with. I had money in those days. It wasn't much — a few thousand dollars. I figured I'd

206

never see it again, but I liked Tom, despite everything. He was a likable sort. And, after all, he was my daughter's husband. And the father of my grandchild.

"Around this time Gallen came out from Chicago. Gallen was a crook, but he was smart enough. He saw that your dad was just the front man he wanted. Personable, a little casual about money. He hired him to front for the operation. Popular fellow around town, just what Gallen wanted as the public face of the business."

"Probably he didn't know all the details of it," I said.

Grampa shrugged. "He wasn't a dishonest man, just weak. The scheme sounded plausible, and he didn't bother to look at it too closely." He pursed his lips. "Then of course the whole thing blew up and he ran."

"What did Mom do then?"

"She was bitter about it, naturally. He'd badly let her down. Let us all down, for that matter."

I remembered what Sonny had said about his mom crying at night in bed. "Did she cry?"

"Not when I saw her. But I imagine she did when I wasn't around."

"Did I cry, Grampa?"

"You were only a couple of years old, remember. You didn't understand it. At first you kept asking, 'Where's Daddy?' Your mom would tell you that he wouldn't be home for a while. Then you began asking if your dad was dead. We'd say no, but he'd had to go away, and wouldn't be back soon. And after a while you stopped asking."

"We never heard anything from him?"

"Actually, we did. After he'd been gone a month or so we began getting letters. Not often, but now and again. He wanted to explain, say how sorry he was, begged us to forgive him. He said he hoped someday something could be arranged so he could get to see us. You, especially—he said he couldn't bear the idea of not seeing his son again. Your mom wouldn't answer his letters. He didn't give an address, of course, but there was a go-between who could have passed letters along. When he realized she wasn't going to answer he phoned a couple of times. Your mom wouldn't speak to him. I talked to him. He begged me to persuade your mom to forgive him. She wouldn't. He wanted

to talk to you, although you were only beginning to talk. She wouldn't let you. After about six
months the letters and the phone calls stopped."

"I wish Mom had let me talk to him."

Grampa shrugged. "It wouldn't matter now,
Gene. You wouldn't remember."

Then Mom came home and we dropped the
subject.

The next morning I felt a whole lot better.
Didn't know why I felt so much better, but
wasn't going to question it. What was the point
in worrying about that voice all the time? When
you got down to it, the specter was right in a
way: he'd gotten a rough deal out of the thing.
Sure, he'd been swindling people, there wasn't
any question about that. But like Grampa said,
they'd brought it on themselves because they
were willing to believe whatever they wanted to
believe. Allowed themselves to get swindled,
you could say. I could see where the specter had
a point. Grampa would be the first to say that
there were always two sides to a question.

I was feeling a little more like swinging a
baseball bat again, so after school Sonny and I
rounded up about ten kids and we went over to

the field where we played. Five to a side—
pitcher, shortstop, first baseman, and two out-
fielders to each team. No leading off, no
stealing. It was nice. Took my mind off all that
other stuff. Why was it my business to worry
about Grampa, anyway? Let him look out for
himself. I liked swinging a baseball bat. I got a
double and a triple, made a couple of nice
stops. By five o'clock, when the kids had to
start home for supper, I was feeling pretty
good. I picked up my bat and slung my glove
over the butt end.

Sonny gave me a look. "You taking your bat
home, or what, *Yew*gene?"

I laughed. "It's okay, Sonny. I need to put
new tape on the handle. I'm not going to slug
anyone with it."

"Maybe I better take it, Gene. Just in case."

"Nah. Don't worry. Nothing's going to happen." I was feeling happy.

"You sure?"

"Sure," I said. "I'm sure."

"Well, okay." But he looked doubtful.

"Don't worry," I said. "I'm okay." I headed
on home, letting the breeze dry the sweat from

my forehead, feeling pretty good. As I walked along I remembered the feeling I'd got when I'd hit the triple a half hour before, the sharp click and the solid feel in my hands. I took the bat off my shoulder and swung it a couple of times. I had a nice groove. If you hit somebody with a swing like that they probably wouldn't feel a thing. They'd be dead before they knew anything about it. Snap, just like that. Grampa most likely wouldn't feel anything at all. One second there, the next second gone.

So I walked on, feeling pretty cheerful and comfortable. It was nice to feel good for a change, after everything I'd gone through. In fact, I felt sort of outside myself, somewhere above my head, maybe, kind of looking down and watching myself walking along taking practice swings with the bat. Somehow, I was in both places — down there, swinging the bat, and above myself, watching. A funny situation, but kind of nice. I chuckled a little about it.

Pretty soon I saw our house ahead. Grampa's car was not parked out front, which probably meant that Mom had gone off with it somewhere. She drove it more than Grampa did, as far as that went. Shopping, maybe. Or at some meeting.

Where was Grampa? He could be in his usual chair by the front window, could be talking on the telephone, could be doing some cleaning to help Mom out. He could be anywhere. So instead of coming in the front door as usual, I slipped along the side of the house, ducking down when I went past the windows.

When I got to the back of the house I took a quick peek through the kitchen window. Grampa wasn't in the kitchen mopping or sweeping. I slipped a little farther to the back door and eased it open a crack. Some music came drifting out. That probably meant that Grampa was listening to some symphony on the radio. That was good: the music would keep him from hearing anyone creeping into the house.

I was still hanging in the air watching myself. It was fun to be two places at once, and I chuckled again. It wasn't likely that Grampa could hear the chuckle over the music.

Grampa's chair was always half turned away from the front window, so he could get good light for reading but look out the window, too.

The best thing would be to slip into the kitchen, and on down the little hall to the living room. He'd be half turned away from me—might not notice me come in, especially if he were concentrating on the music. If he did notice me, he wouldn't think anything of it, anyway, if I walked around in back of him. Afterwards I'd take the money out of his wallet, take some of Mom's jewelry from the box on her dresser. It wouldn't take more than a couple of minutes, I figured.

But I knew I'd better get a look at Grampa to know exactly where he was sitting, which way he was facing, so I'd be able to come up behind him without him noticing. Of course it wouldn't really matter if he saw me come in with my baseball bat and glove—he wouldn't think anything of that. Maybe he would start a little conversation about how the Cardinals did yesterday. Last conversation for Grampa. And I'd answer something and casually walk around behind him.

Still, it would be better to know exactly where he was. So I slipped along the back of the house, keeping my head below the windows, until I'd reached the side window of the living room. I rose a little and took a quick look in. Grampa was sitting with his back to the front windows so as to catch the light, reading the newspaper. It gave me a kind of funny feeling to see him sitting there, the same old Grampa I'd known all my life, who'd taken us in when hard times came, who'd looked after me, taken me to baseball games and such. Kind of hard on him to have something like this happen to him.

Then I reminded myself that he deserved it. I slipped back around the house the way I'd come to the kitchen door. I eased the door open and started to slip forward. Then somebody jerked me from behind and pulled me backwards off the kitchen steps. I went down hard on my back. The bat was snatched out of my hand.

Chapter 12

Sonny was kneeling on my chest, the bat raised over my head. "*Yew*gene, if you don't lay still I'm gonna bust you with the bat."

I lay there feeling dazed and bewildered. I was breathing hard, trembling, and felt weak and sweaty. I remembered well enough what I'd been doing, remembered taking swings with the bat, peeking in at the kitchen door, being outside myself—remembered it all. Yet it didn't seem possible that it was me who had done all that. How could it have been? How had it all happened? Had I become somebody else? I took a deep breath and shook myself all over.

Sonny was staring down at me. "How you feeling, Gene?"

"I feel terrible. Awful."

"I reckoned you might."

I looked into myself for a minute. "I think I'm okay now, Sonny. You can let me up."

He was wary and went on looking at me. "I don't know if I believe you anymore, Gene. You sure you ain't still got the specter in you?"

"Yes. I'm okay. I'm over it."

He went on holding the bat over me. "You sure?"

"I'm sure." Sonny got up off me, but he stood only a couple of feet away, holding the bat. I knelt up and wiped the sweat off my face with my sleeve. "What made you come along, Sonny?"

"You oughta have seen the look on your face when you started off home, *Yew*gene. You was grinning with a smile this wide, and chuckling and jiggling around all excited. I never seen you like that before. Something had got hold of you, I could see that clear enough. I figured I better follow you home."

"It was the strangest thing, Sonny. I was somewhere outside of myself, watching what I was doing. It seemed like fun, kind of interesting, like I was watching a movie."

"It ain't no movie. It was real enough. I never seen no one like that before."

"I've got to sit down, Sonny. All the steam's gone out of me." I sat down on the kitchen stoop. I was feeling dead tired and shaky. "It must have been like that with your dad, Sonny. Just seemed real interesting to him to walk off that lumber platform into midair."

"You think that's the way it was for Mr. Samuels, too? Just seemed real interesting to drive into a tree?"

"I guess so," I said.

Then I heard a car drive up out front. In a minute Mom came into the kitchen and saw us out back. She swung the kitchen door open. "What's the matter, boys? Something wrong?"

I jumped up. "Nothing wrong, Mom. Just tired from playing ball."

"I got to go," Sonny said. "Mrs. Richards, better keep an eye on Gene." And he went off around the house, carrying the bat.

"What did Sonny mean by that?" Mom said.

"Nothing," I said. "I was feeling a little sick after we played ball and he walked me home. I probably ought to go to bed early tonight."

She nodded. "It's been hot. You might have got a little heat exhaustion."

"I think I'll lie down for a while before supper," I said.

"That's probably a good idea, Gene. I don't often see you looking this drained and gray."

So I went up to my room and lay on my back on my bed, staring at the ceiling, waiting, for I knew the specter would come. And in five minutes I began to feel the familiar tightening in my chest and the little animal movements in my gut. "I knew you would come," I said.

"I'm not very happy about what happened, Gene. Not very happy at all."

"I don't care what you think," I said.

"You should have been more cautious. You should have realized that Sonny might suspect something when you went home with the bat. I'm very angry about this, Gene."

I didn't care anymore. "Be angry," I said. "I don't care what you do anymore. Do what you want. Nothing matters to me."

"I think I can make things matter, Gene."

"Are you going to make me do it all over again?"

"No, I don't think so. I might try something different this time. For the sake of variety, you understand. The spice of life. We don't want to do the same thing over and over, do we, Gene? Very boring. Not much amusement in it. So long as there's a little blood splashed around. I must be satisfied, you know."

"Whose blood? Grampa's?"

"No. Not him again. Somebody else, I think."

"Who, then?" I said.

"I haven't decided yet. There are several people I can think of."

"Me? Is it me?"

"You said that, not me," the voice said.

"What are you going to do? Make me dive in front of a car? Take poison? Walk into midair from a high window just because it seems like an interesting thing to do?"

"Did I say it was you? Perhaps there's somebody else who might satisfy me."

I lay there thinking. "Who else? It has to be me."

"It's true that I'm very angry with you, Gene," the voice said. "But perhaps I can think of someone more satisfying."

"I don't care," I said. "It doesn't matter to me. Do what you want. Just go away and leave me alone."

"For the moment, yes. Then we'll see." And it was gone.

I dozed off. Around eight o'clock I woke up. I knew I had to pretend everything was normal, so I went downstairs. Grampa and Mom were in the living room listening to *Amos 'n' Andy*. "How do you feel, Gene?" Mom said. "I decided not to wake you up for supper."

"Better," I said. "I think it must have been the heat."

Grampa was looking at me carefully. He knew from the conversations we'd been having that it wasn't heat exhaustion, but he couldn't figure out what it was. "I can see you need a good night's sleep, Gene."

"You should eat something," Mom said.

I wasn't hungry, but I didn't feel like arguing. We went into the kitchen and I ate a peanut butter and jelly sandwich and drank a glass of milk while Mom sat and watched. Then I went on up to bed. I didn't think I would be able to sleep, but in fact, for the first time in a couple of weeks, I felt kind of relaxed. Sad, but relaxed. It was over. I wasn't going to fight anymore. I was sick and tired of the whole thing. Let the voice do what it wanted. If it wanted me to dive in front of a car, I'd do it, just to get it over with. And I slept through the night and didn't wake up until I heard Mom and Grampa moving around in the kitchen, getting breakfast.

I got up and went downstairs. I was feeling a little better—not so sad and washed out. I was hungry, too—ate a big bowl of oatmeal and two pieces of toast, and that picked up my spirits a little more. I wasn't feeling like my old self, not by a long shot. But I wasn't quite so ready to give up as I had been.

I had got my schoolbooks and was giving Mom a kiss good-bye when there came a knock on the door. Grampa went to answer it. In a moment he came back. "It's Sonny and Sam," he said. "They wanted to see if you were okay."

That made me feel even better. I went to the door. They were standing by the stoop. "I'm okay," I said.

We set off for school. "Sonny told me about it," Sam said. "Was it awful?"

"Not when I was doing it," I said. "At the time it seemed kind of funny. Something to laugh about. I can't figure out how the specter makes you feel that way, but it does." I shook my head. "Afterwards I felt awful."

"Do you think it's going to make you try it again?" she said.

"He said he wouldn't. He said he wanted to try something different. Go after somebody else. I figure it's going to be me, but the specter said he hadn't made up his mind. He said it might be somebody else."

"Who?" Sonny said. "Did he mention any names?"

"No. He likes to keep you guessing."

"It could be one of us," Sam said.

"Maybe," Sonny said. "But he already took care of my dad and your dad, so I reckon it's Gene's family's turn."

"We've got to do something," Sam said. But then we got to school and didn't have a chance to discuss it anymore.

Sam had Girl Scouts after school. I wasn't ready to go over to Snuffy's, and I sure didn't feel like playing baseball—didn't want to hold a baseball bat in my hands for a while.

"What are you gonna do?" Sonny said.

"Try to talk to my dad," I said.

"I didn't think you knew how to call him."

"I don't. But I think he can hear me if I talk to him."

Sonny gave me a look. "You sure about that, Gene?"

"No. I'm not sure. But I think so. I'm going to try it. It's the only thing I can think of."

However, I didn't feel like going home, either. So instead I wandered along through town to the park, climbed up onto the bandstand, and sat down on one of the benches that went around the sides. There was nobody close by—nobody on the bandstand, nobody near. Off in the distance some mothers sat on park benches with baby carriages in front of them. A couple of little kids were playing in a sandbox a ways off.

Then I noticed a man sitting on the bandstand benches about fifteen feet from me, watching me. I was startled, because I hadn't seen him come up, hadn't heard any footsteps. There was something strange about him: he seemed a little faint, not quite clear and solid, as if he were made of lightly colored air. Nice-looking fellow, I thought, maybe thirty-five years old or something, with a neatly trimmed mustache and brown hair that was going back at the forehead. Dressed well—shirt and a necktie, a shine on his shoes, at least as far as I could make out, for everything about him was a little vague and hard to see.

"Hello, Gene," he said. His voice was a little light like the rest of him.

"Dad?" I said.

"I tried to phone you the other day, but you weren't home. I wanted to talk to you before it was too late," he said.

"How did you know it was me sitting here?"

He chuckled. "You'd be surprised. I've seen you a few times before."

"What? How?"

"Oh, I got back to St. Lou from time to time for one reason or another. Business, mostly. Sometimes I'd drive out to Magnolia and have a look around. I usually knew where to find you."

"Out at the field where we play ball, I guess."

"That's it. I'd sit in the car and watch for a while. I saw you hit one into the trees once. It made me feel mighty proud. Sometimes I'd take a few pictures."

"Why didn't you come over and say hello, Dad?"

"Lot of reasons. I wasn't too happy about how things worked out for me in Magnolia. A lot of people here wouldn't want to see me around. I didn't want to stir up trouble for you and your mom. I'd caused you all enough trouble as it was."

"I wish you had come over and said hello, Dad. You wouldn't have stirred up any trouble for me."

He didn't say anything for a minute. Then he said, "Well, maybe. Maybe I should have. But I don't know as it wasn't for the best this way. I'm not sure as I was cut out to be a family man. You've got Grampa. He's been pretty good to you."

I wasn't sure if I ought to ask, but I wanted to know. "Dad, what happened with that oil swin—oil business. Did you know there wasn't any oil there?"

He chuckled again. "No, Gene. I didn't know. I believed in it. Of course, I ought to have looked into it harder. Ought to have done a little more investigating into Gallen. But I didn't. You know how it is—sounds great and you don't want to think that there might be something wrong with it, so you don't."

"Gallen fooled you, too."

"I suppose I fooled myself. You do something stupid, it usually costs you. I can't say he deserved what he got, that wasn't right. But if he hadn't been out to take money from people who couldn't afford to lose it, none of it would have happened."

"Dad, what am I going to do about him?"

"Gene, that's what I've come to tell you. You don't have to worry about him anymore."

"I don't have to worry about the voice?"

"No. Where I am now, I can take care of him. I'll see that he doesn't bother you. You won't hear from him again."

"Or Grampa?"

"No. He won't bother any of you. I can see to it now. I couldn't before, but I can now." He looked at his wristwatch—or so it seemed, from the way he turned up his arm, for I couldn't make out the watch very clearly. "My time's up, Gene. I have to go."

"Will you come back again?"

"I don't know, Gene. I'd like to. But it won't be up to me. We'll see." Then he began to fade away and in a moment he was gone.

I had an awful lot to think about, and for a long time I sat there on a bench on the bandstand, just looking around at the trees rustling in the breeze, the sounds of little kids in the sandbox shouting, watching the birds swoop and dart here and there. Slowly it began to get dark, and I realized that I'd better get home.

So I walked on through town, down our street, and into the house. Grampa was sitting in his easy chair. Mom was sitting on the sofa. She had a handkerchief balled up in her hand and her eyes were red. "Gene, sit down," she said. She patted the sofa beside her. "We have something to tell you."

Grampa nodded. "Gene, we have some bad news."

"I already know," I said. "Dad's dead."

They stared at me. "How'd you know that?"

"I just know."

They didn't say anything for a minute. "A friend of his out there in California called a half hour ago. A buddy of your dad's. He knew all about us, he said, because Tom talked about us to him from time to time. He found our phone number in your dad's phone book. Your dad was killed in a car accident. This fellow said that he was driving along one of those highways they have out there, perfectly clear day, traffic not particularly heavy, and he went off the road. Hadn't been drinking, hadn't had a blowout."

I looked at them both. "You and Mom think he committed suicide, don't you?"

Nobody spoke for a moment. Then Grampa said, "A lot of people are going to think that, Gene. But we needn't. We don't know."

"He didn't commit suicide," I said.

"How can you be sure, Gene?" Mom said.

"I am sure. I know."

They looked at each other and decided to drop it. "Gene, this fellow, this friend of your dad's, said he found a few pictures he was going to send us. A picture of you and your mom when you were a baby. And some pictures of you playing baseball. I can't imagine how he got them."

"He used to visit Magnolia sometimes," I said. "He used to watch me play ball. Sometimes he took pictures."

They stared at me. "Gene, that can't be right," Mom said. "He may have had one or two old friends here he kept up with. They might have sent him pictures."

"No," I said. "He took them himself."

They didn't say anything for a minute. Then Grampa said, "Gene, your mom wants to have a little service for your dad at the church tonight. Do you want to go?"

"Yes, I want to go."

"It'll be private," Mom said. "Just us. I don't think many of your dad's old friends are still around here."

What she really meant was that there were still people in Magnolia who hadn't forgiven him. "That's fine," I said. "Just us."

. . .

When we got home from the service, Mom put out some cake she had made and we sat in the kitchen eating cake and drinking iced tea. "Mom, can we talk about him now?"

"Yes, I guess there's no harm now."

"What was he like?" I asked. "A kind of happy-go-lucky guy?"

"Oh, yes," Mom said. "He was fun, Gene. He was always fun. But there was no future with him because it was always now, it was never tomorrow. That was fine when we were courting and weren't thinking about the future. We were young—I was eighteen years old. But then we married, you came along, and here came the future, ready or not. Oh, Gene, I was tempted to take him back a few times. I knew you ought to have a dad. But it would have been the same old thing again. I didn't think any of us needed that."

So that was the end of it. Or almost the end.

A couple of weeks later Sam and Sonny and I were down at the bandstand wasting time. Sam said, "They're going to condemn the old Toffey place and tear it down. At least my dad says they are."

"How come?" Sonny said. "I kind of like thinking of that noose and them bones lying out there watching the sun go down and the moon come up every night."

"Well, they're going to. Dad says there aren't any bones and noose out there and never were. He said we could go and look for ourselves."

"Well, if they ain't there, they must have flew off by themselves," Sonny said. "They was out there once, plain enough."

"Somebody took them," Sam said.

"Somebody took them?" I asked.

"Yes," Sam said. "And I know who did it, too. Dad and Gene's grampa. They went out there, cut down that noose, and buried the bones, clothes, everything."

"How do you know that, Sam?" I said.

"The day after Dad got his cast off he told Mom he had to see Judge Adamson. He drove off. He came back a couple of hours later. I happened to be looking out the window when he got out of the car. He was carrying a shovel and a pick, and a big knife was sticking out of his back pocket. I'll bet you dollars to doughnuts that those bones and that noose aren't there anymore. Your grampa and my dad buried them."

"So they're gonna keep the thing covered up?" Sonny asked.

"I guess they figured now that we knew they had to. They were afraid we might talk about it with other kids. Word would get out, and people would start talking whether they knew anything about it or not."

"That's so," Sonny said. "Especially if they didn't know anything about it. They're usually the ones who are sure they got facts right."

"Are we going to drop it?" Sam said.

"I think so," I said.

We thought about that for a minute. Then Sonny said, "Know what? I'd like to go out there, find where they buried them bones, and dig a couple of them up. I think I got a right to a little souvenir of it. Nothing too grand — no skull or nothing like that. Just a little finger bone, toe bone. Might make a nice ornament for a key chain, if I ever own anything worth locking up."

So we agreed that we might do that someday. And we might. But I didn't think we would.